CENTER
STAGE

Written By Dana Burkey
Edited By Brittany Morgan Williams

I would like to dedicate this book to Mackenzie! Knowing that my books have ignited your passion for reading is a truly amazing! I hope you enjoy this book as much as the rest of the series.

I would also like to say a big thank you to Sweet Angel Dream Bows for the amazing bow featured on the cover of the book. Thank you for helping my dream bow for this book become a reality!

CHAPTER 1

"Alright Max, whenever you're ready."

I nodded at the assistant coach that had spoken, then stepped onto the blue spring loaded floor in front of me. Standing on the white line representing the edge of the performance space, I took a deep breath, closing my eyes as I let out a long exhale. I shook out my hands, mostly to get rid of the extra nervousness and jitters I was feeling. Then, I opened my eyes and focused them on the spot across the mat where I would land. Finally, I took off to perform the moves I had been working on for the last three weeks in the gym.

Once I had taken a few running steps forward I slammed my feet down at the same time and used the momentum to flip myself over in a front flip more commonly known as a punch front. As soon as my feet hit the ground I pushed off and performed a round off before flipping my body over once again in a back handspring. With the speed and height I had built up I was able to keep my body straight for two more flips. Since my body wasn't bent at the knee the flips were known as whips and gave me the power I needed for my final skill. Pushing with my legs as hard as I could, I performed another back flip, however this one included two twists of my body before I landed on my feet. Known as a double full, the move was the perfect difficult ending to my tumbling pass.

"Great job!" Someone called out, but I was too busy breathing a sigh of relief to figure out who it was. It didn't help that there were also a few people clapping and cheering for me from around the gym. Not wanting to stay in the spotlight too long, I stepped off the mat and allowed the next cheerleader to perform their tumbling pass.

"How did it look?" I asked my best friend as I walked towards her and took the water bottle she was handing me.

"Your height on the double full was the best I've ever seen it," Lexi said honestly. "I think you could have added a kick and still landed it. You should try it on your next pass."

"I don't know about that." I drank a little more water then wiped the sweat off my face. When I pulled my hand away and saw the smudge of eyeliner I turned to Lexi with a frustrated look. "This is why I said no makeup."

"Come on," she laughed, then grabbed my arm and pulled me a few feet away into the bathroom.

Walking to the mirror I was happy to see that I had only smudged the thin layer of black eyeliner a little, and thankfully didn't take off any of my light purple eyeshadow with it. I never wore makeup to practice at the TNT Force cheerleading gym, but Lexi insisted I needed to look good for skill evaluations. After using my finger tips to get the makeup back under control, I stepped towards the sink and wet a paper towel. My face was flushed after the two hours of working out. Although we had just begun the assessment time, like many athletes I arrived to the gym early to finish working on everything I would perform for the coaches and cameras watching.

I patted my face and neck with the wet paper towel, trying to cool off at least a little before walking back out into the gym. My skin was going to stay pink no matter what I did, but at least my hair was in place. This was due to the layers and layers of hairspray I put into my short brown hair while teasing and combing it into a half pony tail complete with a sparkling cheer bow. The bow was one I received once I returned home from Summit, a national cheerleading competition just a month before assessments. There were a few others in the gym that day wearing their custom championship bow, a rather simple bow with the summit logo mounted in the center. But, unlike the other bows, mine represented not just one but two first place wins. My bow had both red and purple glittery fabric surrounding the competitions logo. This was thanks to pulling double duty and performing with two TNT Force Cheer squads, something that was giving me lots of confident going into the new season. After all, I was the first athlete at the gym to walk away from Summit with two first place titles, not to mention I would be getting two championship rings to celebrate as well.

"We need to get back out there," Lexi reminded me, adjusting her red bow in the mirror. It was surrounded by her curled and styled white blond hair.

"I know," I said with a long sigh. "Ready or not, here we go."

"Come on," she laughed. "You are totally ready and you know it."

Shaking my head at her words I simply followed her out of the bathroom and back into the room filled with athletes working to showcase their skills and impress the gym staff. It was the second day of the assessments, the first having been spent learning dances and basic cheerleading choreography. I was happy to say all but a few dance moves were easy enough for me to learn. It was not nearly as bad as the first time I was tasked with dancing on one of the gyms blue mats with an audience watching. There were still a lot of people better than me at dancing, but that's why I was happy for the second day to show my stuff.

Parting ways with Lexi as she moved across the gym to show off her standing jumps, I once again lined up for the tumbling floor. The TNT Force gym was a long and tall industrial room with stark white walls, one of which was covered with mirrors. There were four blue mats making up the length of the room, all with spring loaded floors to help us jump and cheer our best. Between eight rows of mats were a set of cubbies for the athletes to store their gear. Closest to the door were the gym offices, as well as a parent viewing area that was usually filled with adults. During assessments, however, parents were forced to stay outside, and couldn't even peek in thanks to the paper covering the windows. At the far end of the room, farthest from the gym's main entrance, were a series of running tracks, trampolines, and foam pits, all for athletes to use while working on new skills. I had logged many hours over the weeks since Summit making sure I was ready to showcase all that I could do. Now, it was time to show every judge and member of the gym what I had learned.

"Alright Max, you're up," the same coach as before called to me. If I remembered correctly her name was Molly, but since she was a junior level 2 coach I hadn't spent any time with her since joining the gym.

Stepping onto the mat I looked over where Nicole stood on a larger scaffolding style platform set up for the assessments. As both a coach as well as one of the gym's owner, Nicole had coached both of my teams the year before. Around her on the platform were three cameras, used to catch everything occurring on the mats during the night. One pointed towards the stunting mats where girls were lifted and thrown into the air by skilled bases, another was aimed on the standing jump mat where athletes would perform toe touches and hurdlers and back tucks. The final camera was trained on the mat I was about to race across once again. It was my second and final tumbling pass of the afternoon, and I knew I needed to make it count. I realized Nicole was watching me just before I turned away from facing her, and it made me even more confident in what I was about to do. After all, Nicole pushed me to get better and better at cheerleading. And now I could land skills that truly were better than ever.

Taking off across the blue floor I once again began my pass with a punch front followed by a round off. Next, I wiped my body around while twisting, performing a full before my feet met the ground once again. The move slowed me down more than I wanted it to, but I had planned for that. I pushed as hard as I could and used the extra momentum of a back handspring to transition into a whip. That final move gave me the height I needed for the very thing Lexi had encouraged me to do. Kicking my leg up as high as I could, I reached for it with one hand then brought it back down as I immediately began corkscrewing my body, all while flipping through the air. The resulting kick double full was the hardest move I had been working on, and was one I hadn't officially mastered. But, I was determined to land it when it counted, with Nicole and so many others watching. As my feet hit the floor, however, I knew I didn't quite have the force needed. I found myself stepping first one, then another foot forward, then finally falling to my knees. Despite my best effort, I hadn't landed the skill as planned.

I quickly stood up, mad at myself for not sticking to the safer kick single I had been planning before Lexi's encouragements. I turned to walk off the mat, and only then realized people were cheering for me. Glancing towards where the noise was the loudest, I was happy to see that not only were my friends cheering, Nicole was also clapping enthusiastically from her perch with the cameras. Knowing I needed to leave the mat for the next athlete I quickened my pace to a jog, but couldn't help the massive grin growing on my face. Sure, I didn't land the kick double, but based on everyone's reaction they were proud of me. Likely because they knew I was on track to get it soon enough. And that meant that the chance of landing on a top team at the gym was getting more and more possible all the time.

CHAPTER 2

Despite the cheers from everyone in the gym I was still a little disappointed in myself for trying the kick double. It felt good that I was close to landing the hard move, and I knew I would be in the gym for hours and hours to perfect it. But first, I needed to finish the rest of my assessments. After getting some water and stretching for a few minutes I headed to the mat at the far end of the room where I would need to display my skills in the air.

"You ready to fly Max?" Lenny asked. When I nodded to let him know I was ready to fly, he gave me a quick fist bump then called over three athletes that would serve as my bases.

Lenny was a coach that had been gone for the previous competition season while at college. He was back for the summer, and the rumor around the gym was that he was going to be on staff full time for the upcoming cheer season. Although I had only met him twice before the assessments began, I already loved being around him. He was intimidating when you first met him thanks to his large frame and bulging muscles. He had thick dreadlocks to his shoulders and two arms covered with dozens of colorful tattoos that still showed up easily despite his dark skin. On top of that, his face seemed to be in a scowl when he was concentrating, only adding to his overall scary guy image. However, I quickly learned he was the funniest coach at the gym, and knew everything there was about making stunts stay in the air.

A lot of people were working on skills on the large mat, but I found a section that was free just as Connor, Matthew, and Gwen made their way to me. I knew working with them would make the assessment a breeze, considering hours of practice time we had logged together in the gym. We had all been in a skills class together through the winter, so even harder flying skills were becoming second nature for the groups of us. All of that was good for me, considering how I performed would determine if I landed on a level 5 team or not. And a spot on a level 5 team would allow me to finally compete at Worlds, the most coveted international cheerleading competition of the season.

"I want you to do a prep to extension lib, then a basic cradle out," Lenny instructed us with a smirk on his face. He knew we would be able to do the moves in our sleep if we wanted, but it was how assessments worked for flying. We had to start with the basics and move up as we were able. Thankfully it wasn't too long before we were getting to the harder stuff, including level 5 flying that I had only recently mastered.

"I want just Gwen and Matthew to base for this one," Lenny began explaining after trying a few intermediate skills. "I want to see a double around heel stretch, then drop down to prep level out of the skill. Next go back up for a double around to a scorpion. Hold it for three counts then move into a scale. Then I want to see a tick tock lib to a fortune cookie to ground. Connor I want you to step in after that for a basket to end it. Do you want to do a kick single, or go for the double?"

"Double," I said simply, and couldn't help but smile.

As I stood with Gwen and Matthew on either side of me, and Connor spotting us from behind, I realized how strange it was to be standing on the mat about to get lifted into the air. Even a few months ago, I would have needed Lenny to explain everything he had just told me over again and again. But now it was all second nature. I had a clear mental image of every pose and skill he listed, and knew holding them while high up in the air would be something I could accomplish without too much stress. In fact, all of it was so easy that I was back on the ground after completing the whole series of flying skills before I even had the chance to break a sweat.

"You're ridiculous Max," Lenny said with a dramatic eye roll once I was finished. "I don't know why they're even making you try out."

"I think she's just here so the rest of us get used to the idea of having her on one of our squads," Gwen suggested as she pulled her long brown hair into a tighter pony hair complete with a sparkly black cheer bow. "Fingers crossed she makes Bomb Squad."

"No way," Matthew replied. "She's totally going to make Nitro."

"Can we do partner stunts?" I asked Lenny, ignoring my friends play fighting about my team placements.

"Nope, not today," he said with a frown. "They want everyone to do the same series of skills so they can compare. But don't worry. You're going to be doing the one on one skills on a team soon enough."

I nodded, knowing he was likely right. All anyone had been talking about since Summit ended was what team they were going to be on for the following season. After seeing me compete on a junior level 3 and a senior level 4 team on the international stage in Florida, there wasn't a person in the gym that thought I wouldn't be placed onto a level 5 squad. The idea scared me at first, but the longer I started training in the weeks that led up to assessments, the more excited I was for the harder flying and tumbling skills that went with a level 5 team. No one was sure exactly which of the gyms' three level 5 teams I would be placed on, hence the fighting between my two friends.

"That was a great pass you did earlier," Connor assured me. He was walking with me off the mat as Matthew and Gwen continued to go back and forth.

"I didn't land the kick double," I reminded him quickly.

"That doesn't matter," he replied. "No one else all day has even had the guts to try it, let alone almost land it. Well, no one but you."

"Thanks, I think I really needed to hear that."

Connor took the opportunity to stop walking and give me a hug since we had already left the blue cheerleading mat. I was getting more and more used to hugs from my friends at the cheer gym, but sometimes it was strange. This was one of those times. Mostly because it felt like every time I was around Connor he had gotten taller than the last time I saw him. When I joined the gym, he was at least 5'5", a good 8 inches taller than me even then. But, in the few weeks leading up to the end of the season, and in the month since it had finished for good, he had grown at least another 3 or 4 inches. He was starting to push 6 feet, making me feel even more short and tiny next to him. Since, after all, his height also came with more muscles. Thankfully he still looked the same, with his curly dark brown hair, dark green eyes and dimples you could spot from a mile away.

"When are you going to stop getting taller?" I asked Connor as our hug finally ended. "I mean, I know I'm short and all, but now I feel like one of the seven dwarfs next to you."

"You're not that short," he challenged me with a smile. "Besides, you being tiny helped you get thrown extra high for that kick double."

I nodded, knowing he was right. In other sports I played over the years, I was made fun of or seen as a less capable athlete due to always being the shortest and thinnest girls on my teams, even when I wasn't the youngest. But at cheer, everything was different. Being small was a good thing, since you were easier to throw in the air or hold up high off the mat. So, as the smallest 13-year-old at the gym, my size was another thing that would likely help me get placed onto a level 5 squad finally.

"Did you do your jumps yet?" Connor asked as we turned and looked around at the other athletes still performing assessments. The group was slowly thinning out as people finished their skills and headed home.

"Yeah," I said with a nod of my head. "I wanted to get them out of the way first since they're my weakest area."

"You did great, I'm sure," he said before giving me a quick side hug. Then, knowing he needed to get back to basing, he turned and walk back onto the tumbling mat.

Despite being done with my assessments I didn't feel quite ready to head home. That could have been largely because I was used to hours of practice for Blast or Fuze multiple days of the week all last season. Or because of the hours and hours I logged at open gyms since returning home from Summit. Either way, I was free to go, but found myself torn. With all the other athletes still working, it felt strange to just leave.

"Hey Max," Lenny called out to me, as if sensing my hesitation. "Can you come fly for a bit? I have some more athletes that need to try their hand at basing, and you're light enough that even the shorter girls should be able to lift you."

"Okay," I grinned, excited for a reason to stay at the gym longer. Something I never could have imagined thinking even a year ago when I first joined the TNT Force gym.

CHAPTER 3

The following evening I sat in front of the big screen TV in my basement surrounded by more hair products and snacks than I knew what to do with. Thankfully, I was joined by Halley and Lexi who were happy to help devour the junk food, all while forcing the many hair products on me.

"I just want to wear it straight," I stated again. I was still trying to convince my best friends that I didn't need to try their curling methods on my hair for the team reveal in the morning.

"But it will look really cute," Haley begged, complete with a puppy dog face that made her brown eyes look even bigger. "You won't even feel them while you sleep. And if you really hate it in the morning you can re-wash it and straighten it before we leave."

Halley was holding a whole set of the blue foam curlers she wanted me to try. The plan was to wrap my hair in the long foam rods then more or less bend with into place due to the wire in the center of each one. Keeping the curlers in while you sleep would apparently give you beautiful curls when you woke up. Or at least hair good enough for things like team placements. Both of my friends explained that they didn't trust anything but a curling wand for competitions. I agreed with them on that, since before I cut my hair going into Summit I also spend many mornings curling long brown hair. Or rather trying to curl it without burning my fingers too many times.

"What if it looks like a huge puffball?" I asked, leaning away from the hairspray Lexi was holding up to me.

"Just trust us," she whined, giving me her best attempt at a scowl.

"Fine," I finally sighed, knowing they were going to fight me until I gave in.

Both of them let out a squeal before getting to work. Lexi coated my hair in a thick layer of hairspray as 'a base' as they called it. Then, her and Halley each started twisting my hair up into the foam rollers. As they worked, I realized how funny it was that I was sitting at home on a Friday night getting my hair done while having a sleepover with two of my friends from my cheerleading gym. It was normal enough for most girls my age, but for me it was still a fairly new experience.

Less than a year before I had been minding my own business at our towns' trampoline park when I spotted Halley and Lexi doing flips and other tricks. Thinking the various moves looked really cool, I started talking to them, hoping I could learn the flips they were performing. They were my polar opposites, covered in hot pink and glittery clothing while I stood there in old basketball shorts and a stained t-shirt. Not to mention that my messy brown hair was in stark contrast to the well styled light blond hair of both girls. But, despite looking nothing alike, we hung out all day. Then, before I knew it, I was at an open gym time at TNT that the girls, along with Halley's mom, had encouraged me to attend.

TNT Force was a well-known cheerleading gym in Texas thanks to their teams that qualified to the World championships or Summit every year. They hadn't been doing too well at most of the smaller competitions through the season, despite being small compared to a lot of other all star programs in the state. Although, I didn't know all of that when I started at the gym.

Instead I was much more focused on leaving the cheer gym and staying far away from anything cheer related. I was sure no one at TNT would ever accept me for the tomboy I was, so I didn't want to stay long enough to have to deal with standing out. But, with my dad's reminders that my mom was one a cheerleader in high school, years before she died of cancer, and the added bribe of getting two new kittens, I gave TNT Force a try.

Even when I agreed to my dad's terms, I was sure I would never stay at the gym for long. But, when I started to get to know the other girls on Blast, the gyms' junior level 3 team I was placed on, I started to see that cheer was actually pretty fun. When competition season rolled around a few months after I joined the gym, I struggled with not winning every weekend, since I was too competitive to be happy with second and third place time and time again. Thankfully I stuck out the rest of the season, and managed to join a senior level 4 team called Fuze. It allowed me to finish my first season of cheer on a high note, what with two Summit championship wins and all. It also left me excited to begin my second season of cheer, even though I had given up a possible spot on a high-level softball team in the process. In fact, the reminder that I had officially chosen cheerleading over all other sports I grew up playing often pushed me to work even harder on new skills. Something that I was hoping would give me the edge to officially land on a Worlds team.

"So, what exactly is going to happen tomorrow at the team reveal?" I asked my friends, while they were still busy at work with my hair

"No idea," Halley said with a shrug. "It's different every year."

"Well, kind of," Lexi added. "We always get our new practice wear and bows and stuff. And then there is usually an activity or something. Last year we played this crazy new version of capture the flag in the field. It was super confusing but really fun."

"Oh yeah," Halley nodded. "And the year before that we played this big game of soccer using a bunch of yoga balls. The videos from that game were hilarious."

"But how do we find out our teams?" I clarified, although the stories about the games had me excited for what the staff has planned.

"One year they read out the teams and kind of called us up one at a time," Halley explained. "But then there was also a year we all got a scratch off card, kind of like those little lottery tickets. Only when we were told to scratch them, it revealed our team color. Oh, and last year we all had to walk down the mirror wall of the gym until we found our name on these big posters that had the different teams written on them. Whatever they do though, they send all of the e-mails tonight."

"What e-mails?" I wanted to turn to face Halley, but since they were still working on my hair I had to stay perfectly still.

"They e-mail parents to let them know their kids' team tonight," Halley replied, like it was the most obvious answer in the world. "It doesn't list the whole team though, just their child."

"What? Why?"

"So, parents can warn their kids if their team placement is super bad, or even super good." There was a pause, then Halley continued. "If someone was hoping to get on a level 4 team, but they only made it onto a level 3 team, then they might be super upset at the reveal tomorrow. But, if the parents know, they can let their kid know ahead of time and soften the blow. Or, for the little kids, by letting them know ahead of time it keeps them from getting too hyper and anxious and everything."

"My first year at the gym I was so afraid I wasn't going to make a team at all my mom had to sit me down the night before and show me the e-mail before I would even go to bed," Lexi added. "I was so stressed out until I saw proof I was going to get to cheer. I was a total mess."

"But if parents know doesn't that ruin the surprise?" I asked, seeing both the good and bad in letting people know ahead of time.

"Not every parent tells their kid," Halley said simply. "My mom doesn't tell me, but had to tell my sister the year she didn't go up a level like she thought she would. Some people are okay to walk in tomorrow and find out, but other people need to know sooner so they can work on not totally freaking out one way or the other. It really depends on the kids, and the team they make, and their goals for the coming season."

"I guess that makes sense." And it was true, it really did. I had seen the way some of the parents and athletes could be at the gym if they didn't get to be in certain parts of a routine, let alone be on specific squads. It made me glad that I was pretty much guaranteed a spot on a senior level 5 team. Although, as I thought about it more, I began to worry that maybe I could be one of the people disappointed by not getting on the team I wanted.

"Do you think my dad will let me know if I don't make it onto a level 5 team?" I asked, suddenly nervous.

"Do I think he would tell you? Yes," Halley began. "But do I think you'll actually make a non-level 5 squad? No way."

"Agreed!" Lexi said immediately. "I think the only thing that could keep you from cheering on a level 5 team and going to World this year and everything would be an injury. And you're clearly not injured right now based on your flying and tumbling yesterday."

I simply gave my head a little nod in response, my nerves from a moment ago already subsiding. Their support was just one of many things that made me thankful I had them both as best friends. Lexi, who was only an inch or two shorter than I was, was a flier like me. She was always ready to help me improve or push myself when I was trying something new. Halley, who had actually been in my stunt group while I was on Blast, supported me in everything. Literally. She held me in the air while I was flying on the junior level 3 team, but also made sure to give me tips and techniques so when I learned new skills I was performing them perfectly.

I was getting more and more used to having girls as best friends, although I still loved time to hang out with my neighbors Kyle and Peter. Despite the months cheering at TNT Force, I was still a tomboy at my core. I loved running around and playing with the boys next door, who were basically like my brothers. They even tried to support me in my cheer endeavors, although never quite in the same way that Halley and Lexi managed to so often.

"All done," Lexi announced, spraying on a final layer of hairspray before scooting away from me.

Pulling out my phone I held it up to look at my hair in the selfie camera. My hair was wrapped in the blue foam rods, making strange little bumps that looked a little like buns all over my head. For a second I worried I looked funny, but considering my two friends had the same blue curlers in their hair as well helped me feel a bit better about it all. Not to mention we looked more funny than anything since we all matched.

"Selfie," I announced, already trying to image how people would react to the photo on Snapchat.

As my friends leaned in on either side of me I took a quick photo and posted it online right away. For the caption, I added "What would I do without my best friends?" Once I had sent it out, a new thought made me pause instantly. I suddenly realized that in just a few short hours I would officially be on different squads than both Lexi and Halley. Lexi was too young for a senior team still, and Halley didn't have tumbling skills hard enough to make a level 5 squad just yet. I had thought about it before, but in that moment, it hit extra hard. Once I got my team placements the following afternoon, we would officially no longer be teammates. Trying not to let it affect me too much, I pushed the sad though aside and decided it was time for a good horror movie to offset all the hair and makeup time.

CHAPTER 4

Eating three pancakes for breakfast was not a good idea. They sat in my stomach like a brick as we pulled up to the cheer gym and I climbed out of the car with my friends. Much like during the two days of assessments, we were wearing white TNT force tank tops and black shorts that were once so short and tight I couldn't take more than a step without pulling the hem down to make them feel longer. But now, after months of wearing the shorts, I was used to it. I was also thankfully used to wearing makeup and styling my hair around a massive cheer bow. Lexi and Halley had pulled my short bob into a half ponytail to display the plain white cheer bow we were all given on our way out of the gym the day before. It was odd to have an outfit without any of the standard TNT Force team colors on them, but we all assumed it had to do with whatever way they were planning to announcing the team placements.

"You finally made it," Connor said as I walked into the gym with my friends. He gave me a big hug and said hello to Lexi and Halley before we walked in with him to find a seat. I noticed Connor was wearing a white TNT tank top and black gym shorts, matching our look as well. In fact, as I looked around the gym while we waited to find out what was going on, I realized that the only people who were wearing color was the coaches. Sure, the parents had colors on, but they were all standing around the perimeter of the room, while the athletes were told to take a seat on one of the two mats closest to the entrance. The blue mats were a sea of white and black clothing, all worn by a mass of nervous athletes.

The coaches, however, were wearing their team colors for everyone to see. Every squad at the gym had one color that would be featured on their uniforms, cheer bows, and makeup. So, to show who would be in charge of the squads for the year, each coach was wearing their team color, or colors. I spotted Nicole right away. She was wearing a purple shirt to represent Fuze which also featured the TNT force logo in black and red to represent Blast.

Glancing around the room, I saw Tonya and Scott standing next to each other. They were coaches of two of the level 5 teams I might be placed on, so I noticed the hot pink and lime green shirts easily. I was also happy to see that Lenny was wearing orange, showing that he was going to be coaching Spark, the gyms' junior level 4 team. Despite the rumors and talk that he would be coaching now that he was done with college, until I saw his shirt I didn't get my hopes up too much.

I saw a few other coaches I knew a little from open gyms and competition season, but there was one person I was still looking for. Finally, I spotted TJ in his teal shirt as he walked in front of the group of athletes and began to quiet us down. He was one of the gym's owner as well as the coach of Nitro, the same team that Connor was a member of. If all went as planned, I would be cheering for TJ, Nicole or Scott for the new season, finally performing for a level 5 team.

"Let's quiet down everyone," TJ called out, a massive smile plastered onto his face.

"We want to get started with this year's team reveal."

With those words the room went instantly quiet. Everyone stared at TJ, not speaking or moving at all. This was finally the moment we were all waiting for. The moment the last few weeks in the gym had been leading up to. Or, for many people, a moment that they had been anticipating for years. Would this be the year they made the team they had always dreamt of? Sitting there in that moment, only minutes before the results, I was getting more and more nervous by the second. I could feel my palms growing sweaty with nerves as my heart pounded harder and harder.

"First of all, we want to thank everyone for being here this week and committing to another great season at TNT Force," TJ began, his smile still not flattering at all. I got the feeling he was just as excited as all the athletes were. "We have watched and re-watched all of your performances at the assessments. Then, we did our best to put everyone on a team where they can grow and learn as an athlete and showcase their skills and talents the best way possible. Today we are excited to take each squad's first official team photo and also play a fun game to kick off the season. But first, who's ready to find out what team they are on?"

The screaming and cheering was instantly deafening, but excited all the same. I found myself cheering right along with my friends, my nervous excitement at an all-time high. I closed my eyes and took a long deep breath, willing myself to be calm. In fact, I was so distracted trying not to freak out that I didn't even realize what was going on until Halley was handed a large black gift bag.

"What is that?" I asked her pointing to the bag for emphasis.

"Did you hear anything TJ said?" Connor asked, nudging me with his arm.

"Yes," I lied. "But just in case, why don't you remind me."

With a laugh, Connor quickly explained to me that the coaches were going to be handing out the large black gifts bags to everyone. They had our names written on the bags front with silver sharpie, so it was easy to hand the right bag to the right athlete. Once all the bags were given out, we would all get to open them at the same time to reveal our teams for the new season. It wasn't clear exactly what was in the bag, only that it was going to give everyone the hopefully good news.

At first there was a lot of talking and murmuring going on in the gym, as well a lot of parents taking photo after photo. But then, as the last of the bags were set down in front of athletes, the room got quiet. Clearly there were a lot of people, like myself, who didn't get the news from their parents the night before. There was a nervous tension in the air that was building every second. It made me want to rip the white tissue paper out of the black bag and get it all over with. It also made me want to leave my bag with my friends and go stand outside to get some fresh air. Thankfully, TJ began talking again before I could race out of the gym.

"Alright everyone," he began, his smile somehow even bigger than before. "You can open those bags in 3….2….1!"

By the time the word 1 was out of his mouth there was tissue paper flying in the air and screams erupting around the gym. It was so sudden that I wasn't sure what to do in that moment. Instead of pulling the tissue paper out of my bag to find out the news once and for all, I froze. Suddenly, there was just too much to process for me to know how to function. But, in a way, it was nice since it allowed me to see my friends open their bags, while I sat holding the edge of the tissue paper with one hand.

"I'm on Spark," Lexi exclaimed, pulling a black and orange cheer bow from her bag.

"Me too!" Halley squealed, an orange pair of cheer shorts in her hands.

With more squealing and laughing they gave each other a hug, clearly excited to not only be on the same squad, but also to be on a level 4 team. That meant harder stunts, harder tumbling as well as being one step closer to making it to a level 5 team and all that comes with it. The mere thought of a level 5 squad made me turn my attention to Connor who, much like myself, was ignoring his still unopened bag. Instead of checking his team assignment, he was watching me with a strange look on his face.

"What?" I asked him, having to raise my voice over the sound of athletes in the gym celebrating.

"Nothing," he replied. "I just want to see you open your bag already."

"Got it," I nodded. Then, with a deep breath, I pulled out the tissue paper and peered into the large black bag.

With just one glance, all my nerves were ancient history. Instead I was immediately bubbling over with excitement as I reached my arm into my bag. I noticed Halley and Lexi were now sitting quietly as I began pulling an item out, likely watching like Connor was. But their silence only lasted a few more seconds, and was then instantly replaced by more celebrating as they saw the teal bow that I pulled out of my bag.

"You're on Nitro," they both exclaimed. Or at least I assumed that was what they were saying. It was hard to be sure thanks to the super high pitch of their voices.

"Congrats Max," Connor said. It looked like he was about to lean in for a hug when Lexi and Halley more or less tackled me in a big group hug.

Caught up in the moment, I hugged them in return, and found myself having to fight back tears. As much as everyone told me I was going to be on a level 5 team, I was always doubting it at least a little. Realizing I was on Nitro was only part of what struck me in that moment. I was also struck with the knowledge that I wasn't on just any squad. The team bow proved I was on the same team as Connor. Fighting against my friends to sit up, I turned to look at Connor. I wasn't really sure what I should say to him, but he spoke before I could, saying the best words I could imagine hearing in that moment.

"Welcome to the team."

CHAPTER 5

Ignoring the rest of my bag for the moment, I gave Connor a big hug before springing to my feet. My eyes quickly scanned the room, looking to find my dad. When I realized he was walking towards me, I skipped the last few steps between us and leapt into his arms. He caught me, spinning me around a few times before finally setting me back down on the mat.

"Congrats sweetie. I knew you could do it."

"Thanks Dad," I replied easily, my face already hurting from the smile that was still plastered to my face.

I talked to my dad for a moment longer, and of course got a photo with him when a mom nearby offered. Then, I walked over and sat back down with my friends, and decided to go through the rest of the black bag. I had just managed to pull out a pair of teal cheer shorts when Nicole began to quiet everyone down. She used a series of claps that was returned halfheartedly, since many people were still freaking out about their new team. Nicole tried again, and thankfully everyone seemed to catch on. Once the clapping died out she began talking and giving instruction.

"Congrats one and all," Nicole announced. "This year is going to be a great season thanks to all of you, and of course thanks to all of your parents and their dedication to allowing you to cheer here at TNT. We have some more fun planned, but for now we need everyone to find their coach and get ready to take your first official team photo."

Connor stood up, then offered a hand to help me get up as well. Once I was standing Connor kept one arm around my shoulder as we headed towards where TJ was standing near the gym entrance. By the time we reached him there was quite a crowd growing, and I found myself celebrating all over again. I tried to say hello to a few people, but then was picked up off the ground in a massive hug. It startled me at first, but then I saw it was Matthew. As Lexi's older brother, and a member of my skills class with Greg, I was around him a lot. Until I saw him, I hadn't really thought about the fact that I would be on the same team as so many of my friends, not just Connor.

"So, I'll take it you didn't know ahead of time," Connor said me as Matthew finally sat me back on the ground.

"Nope," I said with a shake of my head. "I kind of wish he would have told me. But at the same time, as long as I was on one of the level 5 teams I was going to be happy."

"Well, I'm glad you're on Nitro and not Bomb Squad or Detonators," Connor explained with a smile. "We finally get to be on a squad together. And who knows, maybe we'll even get paired up for partner stunts."

"No way, I'm calling dibs," Matthew chimed in.

They continued to go back and forth, their argument very much like their play fight during assessments. The only difference was that now they were fighting over stunt groups instead of team placements. Ignoring them, I looked around and was happy to see a few familiar faces also standing around me. I recognized a few people that had been on Nitro last season, but I was also happy to see two of my Fuze teammates standing with the Nitro group as well. Juleah, who had been in my stunt on Fuze, along with Taylor who I had met a few times while on the purple team were both a few steps away. I tried to see around people and find out who else might be new to the team, but struggled due to how short I was. All the tall athletes that were near me made it impossible to see past them. Thankfully TJ got my attention when he finally began speaking to the group.

"Welcome to Nitro everyone!" he exclaimed, eliciting a lot of clapping and cheering from all of us. "We just need to take a quick team photo, then we're all heading outside for the game."

Moving towards the front, where I was certain all the shortest athletes would need to stand, I turned and ran right into Leanne. Ever since I had met Leanna just after joining the gym, she always seemed to dislike me. She would find ways to give me back handed compliments, shoot me looks from across the room, or interrupt me while I was talking to Connor or anyone else she was also friends with. It was annoying, but in the past I could walk away and go back to practicing or hanging out with my teammates. As I stepped back and muttered an apology for bumping into her, I realized I no longer had that option. Being on Nitro meant I was now on the same squad as her, and would be more or less stuck with her all season.

I expected a rude remark for the run in but she simply shrugged in reply. Although the gesture wasn't super nice, it was much better than anything she had done or said to me in the past. It made me think that maybe being on the same team would be a good thing. Sure, I knew we didn't have much in common aside from our abilities in cheerleading, but teamwork had to help at least a little bit. Or at least I could hope. Right?

Despite being only a few inches taller than me with a similar small but muscular frame, Leanne I looked nothing alike. Her hair was bleached a white blonde that was always teased and curled and styled high around her cheer bow. As if her hair wasn't over the top enough, she also always wore a thick layer of makeup, even while at the gym for practice. In fact, between her hair, makeup, and dark orange-ish tan I knew came from a tanning bed, she often looked more like a cartoon character than a real person.

Standing next to her for the photo, I was a little shocked when she put her arm around me. It was strange, but I tried to remind myself to not show it too much. There was a small, although it was a small chance, that maybe she had a change of heart after Worlds. I mean, there were a lot of posts online about the fact that her side of the pyramid fell during the final performance. And, as if that wasn't bad enough, there were athletes and parents at the gym that pretty much felt the loss was her fault. Maybe everything she went through was helping her turn over a new leaf. One where she was actually nice to me for a change.

I assumed it would be one quick photo and then we would move on. Instead a whole mass of parents also took out phones and camera and snapped pictures as well, including my dad who was still beaming at me. Their photo taking was followed by a few TNT athletes taking pictures, as well as Nicole. She told us the photo was going up on the gyms' Instagram page, so we had to smile "extra pretty." Thankfully, as the last flash went off we were dismissed to head outside and find our team trash can. The instructions were strange, but as I walked out into the Texas sun, I saw that the field next to the gym was dotted with large trashcans, all labeled with thick stripes of colored duct tape. I walked with the rest of Nitro to the can with teal tape on it, and waited for instructions.

"Listen up everyone," Nicole began after getting everyone quiet. She was standing on top of the same scaffolding from assessments, and was once again surrounded by cameras. "Although you will all be representing the gym, working alongside each other in classes and cheering each other on at competitions, today is all about seeing what team is the best."

Nicole went on to explain that inside each trashcan was colored powder. It was our goal to cover ourselves and everyone around us with as much of our team color as possible. This was of course going to be hard since everyone had that same goal, but all the teams looked up for the challenge. We would have 10 minutes to work at getting the color spread over every athlete in the field, and then a winner would be chosen based on what color covered the most of the athletes and their white gym wear.

"Make sure we have some color left right at the end so we can cover ourselves," a boy I didn't know said after the rules were explained.

"Yeah, and don't use too much powder all at the start," a girl standing next to me added. "The more we save to use later on the better."

I barely had time to register their comments when an air horn went off announcing the start of the 10 minutes. Immediately there were clouds of bright color flying around the field as teams began removing the trash can lids and coating themselves and other people around them in as much as their team color as possible. Within seconds I could feel the powder inside my nose and even in my mouth, but did my best to ignore it as I picked up handfuls of teal and raced after other athletes. Not stopping to even see who I was covering in powder, I threw the color I was holding then raced back for more over and over again. Around me everyone was doing the same thing, making it all but impossible to see in the haze of rainbow powder floating through the air.

I was only vaguely aware of other athletes playing the game, unable to tell my own teammates from members of other squads unless we were at the trash can. The trash can that became more and more difficult to find as time ticked away. Everything around me was so bright and colorful it was hard to tell just what was going on, or if my team was winning. Trying to just focus on spreading the teal everywhere I could, I threw handful after handful, the color also landing on me as I worked.

"Two minutes," Nicole called out much to my surprise. It felt like only seconds had passed, but clearly the cloud of colors was effecting my sense of time.

I squinted to find my way back to the teal trash can, then began spreading the color onto my face and legs. As I was doing so I realized just how much of the other colors were on my body as well. Apparently, I had been so focused on covering others in teal, that I didn't do a good job of avoiding other colors. There were large pink and yellow patches all over my arms and legs, which I quickly tried to cover with powder from my teams' trash cans.

"Here, get my back," a voice said to me between coughs.

I quickly rubbed teal onto the shirt that was almost completely red before turning around for them to return to favor. When they turned, it looked like the person might have been Matthew, but I had no way to be sure. What I did notice, however, was that the air was getting even thicker with the swirling cloud that was turning a greyish brown thanks to each team's powder mixing together.

"Five…. Four…. Three…. Two…One! All color down!"

At Nicole's final words I dropped the last handful of teal I had been holding over my head and waited. Everyone seemed to be looking around in silence, waiting to see the results of our work. The wind eventually carried enough of the colors out of the air for us to see again, and when I did I was shocked. Not only was there a lot of color on each of the athletes, the ground also appeared to be tie-dyed. It was everywhere, even on some of the parents who had been standing a safe distance away to film and take pictures.

"Did we win?" Connor asked, walking over and giving me a smile. His teeth were lime green and purple thanks to the other teams' handy work.

"I don't know," I shrugged, seeing that some teams were covered in teal, while other looks like they didn't have a drop of our color on them at all.

"To help figure out which team won we're going to take team photos again, so stay where you are and wait for your coach to come over for the photo." Nicole explained before climbing off her platform to join her teams for the second round of photos.

TJ joined myself and the other athletes on Nitro, instructing us to stand in the same positions that we had for the first photo we took as a team. We all listened, then stood frozen in our spots while everyone snapped pictures. Standing all together like that it was clear that we were covered mostly in teal thanks to our last-minute strategies. It was also clear that we had other colors on our skin and clothing to show we hadn't gone without attack from the other squads.

As we finished the last of the photos, Nicole stepped back up onto the platform and got everyone's attention with the same claps from earlier. We all clapped in reply, then had to wait as the laughter died down. The act of clapping made more clouds of colors waft into the air.

"Okay everyone, it's time to announce the winner," Nicole called out to us. "After taking a look at all the teams our judges have determined that the winning team is…. Bomb Squad!"

As the pink team cheered and hugged one another, causing a cloud of color to once again explode around them, I found myself smiling. Sure, Nitro didn't win the challenge, but I was still proud of my team all the same. Within just a few minutes after finding out I was on Nitro, I was becoming more and more excited for every part of the season to follow. Before the season could begin, however, I knew it was going to take a lot of soap and shampoo to remove the rainbow of colors from my body. Thankfully the game had been enough fun that it was all worth it.

CHAPTER 6

"How does it look?" I asked walking into the living room Saturday night before bed.

I was wearing the new Nitro team practice uniform that was in the black bag I had received at the team reveal. Not wanting the items to be covered in the colored powder, I didn't bother going through the bag until after I got home and showered. Or rather showered twice since it took that long to get some of the orange and pink out of my hair. Once it looked like I had all the color off my body I went through the bag finally, deciding right away I needed to show my dad the new outfit.

Much like the Blast and Fuze uniforms I had been given when I was on the red and purple team, my basic practice wear was made up of short teal shorts and a black tank top with the TNT Force logo in white and teal glitter in the center. I also had two short sleeve shirts that matched the tank top, all given to me in a teal glitter backpack. There was, of course, also the black and teal tick tock bow that had first alerted me to my place on Nitro. It had "MAX" written in rhinestones, something I didn't notice when I first removed it from my bag. The only other items in my bag were two sports bras, both made of teal fabric covered in sparkles and the TNT Force logo.

When I pulled the sports bras out of the bag I was really confused at first. I expected them to just be teal and black so we could wear them under our uniforms later in the season. But, when I noticed the logo, I had a feeling they were a part of the practice wear just as much as the tank tops. Not quite ready to parade around my house in one of them, I went for the shorts and tank top, my newest pair of cheer shoes and my bow, which was placed haphazardly onto my head.

"You look like a World champion to me!" my dad said snapping a photo before I could stop him. "I need to get online and order a new shirt to match. Can't wear last year's cheer dad shirt in red now that you're on the teal team."

"Right after you delete that photo," I suggested, moving towards him.

"It's just a squeak going on my tweety," he assured me, pushing send before I could stop him.

"It's called a tweet, and it's going on Twitter," I quickly corrected him with an eye roll as I plopped down onto the couch.

"That's what I meant," he grinned, thankfully setting down his phone before he could do any more damage. "So, what are we doing for dinner?"

"Pizza?" I suggested, pulling out my phone to post a selfie to Snapchat wearing my new bow and practice gear.

"Mushrooms and sausage this time?"

"Of course," I nodded. "I'm gonna go change."

"Already?" my dad asked as I got up and started walking out of the room. "Shouldn't you start getting used to wearing your Nitro gear?"

"I have all season for that," I shrugged.

Walking into my room and put on a pair of black basketball shorts and a red t-shirt that announced TNT Force Blast were "Summit Champions, 2016." I had another one in my closet in purple that was for Fuze, but usually chose to wear the red version since it was the team I was on the longest. Although, I realized in that moment, starting the year off on Nitro meant I would end up on it longer than I was even on Blast the season before. Even though I was on Blast for the whole season, since I didn't join the team until August it made my season shorter than it was for other athletes. It meant I joined the team before competition season, but still managed to miss the summer conditioning I heard so much about.

The thought of conditioning in the heat of summer made me instantly want to go for a swim. Knowing it would be a while before the pizza was delivered, I took a second to slip on my one piece green bathing suit. Then, I grabbed a towel from the linen closet in the hallway before making a beeline for the backyard.

"Swimming?" my dad asked, although the answer was pretty clear.

"Yeah, just for a little while. I'll get out when dinner is ready."

My dad nodded then went back to whatever he was doing on his phone, likely posting something random on Twitter. It was his favorite way to stay up to date on the cheer world, and he felt the need to post a few dozen time a day now that he had over 100 followers. I hoped the new post wasn't about me, but didn't worry too much. Especially once I stepped outside and dropped my towel onto one of the deck chairs before jumping into the shallow end of our in-ground pool. I quickly swam to the center of the pool and rolled onto my back to float in the cool water.

"Nitro, huh?"

The sudden voice startled me, causing me to spin my body around and sink under the water before I could recover. I quickly came up out of the water for a breath of air, laughing at myself even as I coughed. Kicking my legs to propel me to the side of the pool, I grabbed onto the ladder and looked up to see extremely familiar dark tan skin, light green eyes, and super curly brown hair that could only belong to Peter. He was standing on the deck with a sheepish smile on his face as he held out a hand to help me out of the pool. His grip, combined with the easily seven inches of height he had on me, allowed him to almost lift me out of the water without use of the ladder. Thanks to my quick exit from the pool, I got sprinkles of water on his khaki cargo shorts and faded black t-shirt, although I was sure Peter didn't mind too much.

"Sorry," he said between his laughter. "Are you okay?"

"Yeah," I nodded, still doing a mixture of laughing and coughing.

"I saw your snap," Peter said as I walked over to grab my towel. "So, you made Nitro?"

"Hopefully," I replied, brushing wet hair off my forehead.

"What do you mean?"

Peter sat on one of the deck chairs and I instantly sat in the chair next to him before answering. "There are a few people that will still get cut from the team I think, so hopefully I'll still be there once we get down to 20 people."

It wasn't something I had thought about much or even told anyone, but it was something I noticed when our team photo was posted online. We had more than Nitro's allotted 20 athletes, meaning a few people were likely going to get cut before competition season rolled around. I waited for Peter to ask more questions or say something encouraging, but instead he simply laughed. I found myself upset for a second, but it was clear he wasn't laughing at me to be rude. Most people might not be able to tell the difference, but after almost 4 years I knew him well. Every facial expression he made and every tone his voice took on was easy for me to read. It came with spending almost every day with him and his younger brother Kyle since I arrived in Texas and moved into the house next door to them. They often felt more like brothers to me than just friends, so I knew instantly Peter was laughing because the idea of me getting kicked off Nitro was just a joke to him.

"Hey, it could happen," I tried, although my voice didn't even convince myself.

"And I could be a cheerleader one day too," Peter challenged.

"That could also happen." My response only made Peter laugh louder. "I feel pretty confident and all, but I don't want to let my head get too big just to get disappointed a few weeks from now."

"If they cut you from Nitro, it would only be to move to Detonators or Bomb Squad," he said evenly, shocking me that he could name all of the other level 5 teams so easily. "Don't look so surprised. I went to enough of your competitions last year to know all the teams at the gym."

"Prove it," I instantly challenged him.

"Okay." Peter rubbed his hands together as if he was getting ready for something much more serious than naming squads at the TNT Force gym. "Flame is the junior 2, Blast is junior 3, and Sparkler is level 4. Then the senior teams are-"

You already messed up," I announced, stopping him. "It's not sparkler. It's Spark."

"Close enough and you know it."

I tried to think of something to say, but couldn't think of a good reply. Peter really did know the competition teams at the gym, and likely knew how good each team was as well. That meant that when he assured me I was going to stay on a level 5 team, he truly believed just what he said.

"Either way, I'm on Nitro for now and it feels awesome."

We sat and talked a little more about my summer team schedule, all the new teal gear I had already gotten, and Peter's upcoming family vacation to California. The conversation was light and easy, like all of my conversations with Peter. Or at least most of them. Right after I got my haircut the week before I headed to Summit, it was like he couldn't be around me. Or at least not without just silently staring at me with this strange look on his face. Thankfully it only lasted for a few days, and after that everything was back to normal.

"You staying for dinner, Peter?" my dad asked, standing in the open patio doorway.

"Only if it's pizza," Peter replied with a grin.

"I'll get a plate out for you then."

"So when do you start practice with Nitro?" Peter asked after sending a text to his parents that he was staying for dinner. It happened often enough that I was certain they weren't even a little surprised.

"Monday," I said, instantly feeling nervous excitement building at the thought of it.

"Well, just try not to show off and make the other cheerleaders feel too inferior on the first day," Peter suggested with a grin.

In reply I simply rolled my eyes then stood up to head inside. I wanted to change before dinner, so it was a good excuse to not answer Peter in the moment. He was trying to act like I was super important to the team, but I knew that wasn't the case. Or rather, it couldn't be the case. As a new flier to a level 5 team, I knew there was likely many people better at conditioning and the overall skills compared to me. There was a chance that by the end of the season I might be a 'top' member of the team. But, walking in from last season's level 3 and 4 teams, I knew I would have to work hard to keep a spot on Nitro. No matter what Peter or anyone else thought.

CHAPTER 7

"Slow down Max, you're going to make the rest of us look bad," Matthew gasped Monday afternoon as we ran laps around the block of the TNT gym.

"Sorry," I shrugged, while slowing my pace only a little. "I figure the sooner I get done the sooner I can sit down and stop running."

"Well, try to make it look like it's at least a little hard for you, for my sake," he tried again. He was now practically matching my pace. I slowed a little to help.

When Monday rolled around I was excited to head to the gym for my first Nitro team practice. Since it was still before my dad got off work, I biked to the gym wearing my teal shorts, new bow with my name on it, and a tank top covering the bedazzled sports bra. The idea of wearing even less clothing while I was being lifted into the air or tumbling was not something I was eager to try. I assumed others would feel the same way. But, when I arrived to TNT Force I was a little shocked to see how many of the girls at the gym were wearing just the sports bra. Or at least I was shocked until I realized what they likely already knew. Summer conditioning was no joke.

The first big time chunk was spent going over the schedule for the next few weeks, allowing each person to introduce themselves and share a few things so we could all get to know each other. I was happy to see there were a lot of other new members to Nitro, many of whom had also moved up from either level 3 and 4 teams like myself. Learning more about TJ was also great, since I began to see how fun he was going to be. Nicole was always stern and serious in the gym, but from stories I heard from Connor as well as what I saw from him at competitions, it was clear that TJ was a super fun coach. Not only was he always laughing and joking with people, he took team spirit to the next level with his hair. It was dyed teal, something I soon learned was a start of season tradition everyone always looked forward to.

The hair might not have looked great on other people, but it worked on TJ. He was tall and thin, although still muscular from years of cheerleading. He had a super angular face, and eyes that perfectly matched his teal hair, although it was naturally a dirty blonde. TJ's new hair, combined with his teal TNT Force shirt complete with the same rhinestones that were decorating the shirts of all the athletes on Nitro, made his overall look a lot to take in. His fun personality simply shone for everyone to see, although once we 'got to work' it was hard to remember the less serious side of him. That was in large part due to his plan for conditioning even the returning members of the team weren't quite ready for.

"Look, we're almost done," I told Michael, picking up my pace once again as I turned the corner. It was the fifth lap, bringing the start of practice running total to 3 miles. "Wanna race?"

"Not even a little," Matthew managed, slowing down even more as he pushed his sweat soaked white blond hair out of his face. When I didn't slow down as well and instead began to pull ahead he simply called after me, "Show off."

"Of course you're back first," TJ laughed, handing me a frozen otter pop as I walked back into the gym.

"Thanks," I said taking the treat. "What's next?"

"A break," he replied. "It's going to be a little while until everyone else is back."

With a shrug, I sat down on the blue mat and enjoyed the orange pop I was holding. I was joined by Matthew within a few minutes, and then others slowly began to trickle in. Unlike when I arrived, they all but threw themselves onto the floor and gobbled down their icy treat like it was all that was keeping them alive. Thankfully, after sitting and resting, everyone caught their breath and began to talk.

"Why are we going so hard on day one?" Connor asked, taking a long drink from his teal TNT water bottle before continuing. "I feel like last season we actually built up to stuff like this."

"It wasn't that hard," I shrugged, then instantly regretted it.

"We didn't all spend the weeks off training," Leanne replied, overhearing my comment as she was walking past. It was accompanied with an eye roll, something I was beyond used to seeing from her.

"Really? You guys weren't training even knowing assessments were coming?" This was said only to my friends sitting on the mat around me, since Leanne was thankfully no longer within earshot.

"TJ knows what we're capable of, so if we miss a pass or don't quite perform at our best at assessments then we know we'll still make the team," Matthew explained. "It's good to still stay more or less in shape, but after Worlds is the one month out of the whole year that we don't have to be constantly training."

"Not that we think you training is a bad thing really," Connor quickly same to my defense.

"Speak for yourself," Matthew laughed. "I'm a good runner, and she totally smoked me. I have a rep to protect and if I let little Max here beat me I'm going to be made a fool of fast!"

"I think you do enough of that on your own," Emma, Matthew's girlfriend, quickly interjected.

The two of them began their usual flirt-fighting as Lexi called it, so I took the time to stretch. It felt good after the run, and I knew it would help me once we got started on skills. Although, I didn't know exactly what those skills would entail for the first day of practice.

Either way I wanted to be ready no matter what.

"Two minutes people," TJ called out.

"I think your enthusiasm is great," Connor said, leaning in closer to me while Matthew and Emma went back to their conversation.

"Thanks," I grinned, glad to have Connor by my side.

Aside from Lexi and Halley, he was my best friend at the gym, so knowing I was on the same squad as him was nice. Being on a team with Lexi and Halley would have been better, but I was hoping it wouldn't be too long before I got to know more people on Nitro. Having our names on our bows helped with that allowing me to feel like I knew people a little the first time meeting them. That was exactly the case when a gift with poker straight black hair and tan freckles skin sat down next to me. After taking in her blue green eyes and nose ring I saw from her bow that her name was Jade.

"So, Max, are you ready for some real level 5 skills?" Jade asked.

"Totally," I nodded. "It's just not the same trying things in classes, so I'm really excited."

"Well, we won't quite get to the real stuff today," Jade added with a frown. "We have to build up to that while we find out stunt groups and partner stunts and everything."

Before I could ask more, TJ launched back into practice. It began with all of us finding a spot on the mat, lining up on the tape that held the seconds of the mat flush together. TJ instructed the shortest people to stay near the front of the lines, so everyone could see over the people behind them. It was similar to the way we would line up on Fuze and Blast, so I stayed near the front as everyone else shuffled around. I knew I was short, although it wasn't until we were all in place that I saw just how short I was.

Looking around, I saw that Matthew, Connor, and all of the taller bases were in the back. In front of them were a lot of more averaged height people, including both Emma, Jade, and Juleah who had been in my stunt team while I was on Fuze the year before. Then, closest to me were other girls that were considered short by all standards. In fact, I realized as I was looking at the other four girls in the front line with me, I was the shortest by a few inches. Leanne was next in height, although it was hard to tell just how much taller than me she was. This was mostly since her hair was teased and piled so high on her head around her bow, it made her look taller than even the girl behind her. Either way, I was the shortest of the short girls, and more than likely the youngest person on the squad as well. I was used to it thanks to my time on Fuze, but it was still a little strange after a whole season on Blast where I was surrounded by a lot of other short and younger athletes as well.

"Okay everyone," TJ called out once we were all in place. "We're doing 10 reps in each set, and doing 5 sets of each. Jumping jacks, sidekicks, and front kicks. After that we're moving on to pushups, planks, crunches, squats, and then some standing jumps."

As others around me let out a groan I tried to stay positive. The run was long, but not too difficult. Conditioning would likely be the same. Or at least that was the hope I held onto through the beginning exercises. Much like on Blast and Fuze they were sharp and angular versions of motions most people were used to. So, they were easy enough while still challenging athletes to flex their muscles and "lock their core," as Nicole always used to say when I first joined the gym.

"I hope you're not tired yet," TJ commented as we finally got ready to move into the pushups, planks, and more. Around me, I could see a few people looked pretty tired; sweat was already dripping off of them. I was basically doing okay, although the heat was a lot to overcome, even with the large gym fans running. My only hope was that we were almost finished for the day. As if reading my mind, TJ added, "I hope no one is tired yet. We're just getting started people."

CHAPTER 8

Although I believed TJ when he hinted at how hard the practice was about to become, it in no way prepared me for how true the statement actually was. We went through a series of conditioning exercises that were difficult for everyone, to say the least. We did bear crawls around the mat, we crab walked from one side of the floor to the other, we did lengthy wall sits, and we even did candlestick back tucks. Adding in the extra movements before the back tuck made it extra hard, not to mention it was after all the other drills. It made landing the basic flip much more strenuous than usual. What really got me feeling bummed, however, was that thanks to the conditioning we never got around to working on flying or even running tumbling.

"I don't get it," I said to my friends the next morning as we sat around my pool. Halley and Lexi had come over to swim for a while before they had their first Spark practice at the gym. "Why would we start doing things that hard and not even do any real cheerleading?"

"Sounds like TJ's already getting ready for Worlds," Halley commented, while Lexi nodded in agreement.

"But Worlds is almost a whole year away," I reminded them. "We won't even have a shot to quality until at least December."

"True," Lexi nodded. "But if you work hard enough now, when you get more into the season you will have a lot of stamina. The Worlds teams do it every year, just maybe not to this level."

"Yeah," Halley went on. "This intense conditioning is kind of normal Nitro. Just a little bit more sooner than most years.

"So you mean we're going to have to do that stuff all the time?" I groaned.

"Aren't you so glad you're on Nitro now?" Halley teased.

As much as I wanted to agree that it was nothing but a bummer, I knew it wasn't true. The hard work would get easier eventually. I hoped it was sooner rather than later, but until then I could at least be happy with the fact that I survived. Especially since there were a few athletes that didn't make it through the hard conditioning without throwing up. Not to mention the number of people that had been on Nitro the year before were admitting just how exhausted they were compared to in seasons past. It was a small consolation to know I fared pretty well compared to some of the other athletes on my new team. But, then again, if I wasn't better than at least a few of them, then I had no shot at staying on Nitro in the long run.

"Matthew said you and Connor hung out after practice was over," Lexi stated, although it sounded more like a question.

"Yeah, he walked home with me since it's on his way," I explained easily. "I didn't get to ride my bike, but he helped wheel it for most of the way so that was nice."

"He lives 20 minutes away," Halley corrected me. "On the opposite side of town. After he walked you home he still had to go back to the gym and wait for his mom to pick him up."

"Maybe he was worried I was too tired to make it home on my own," I guessed. "Or had extra time to kill."

"Maybe," Lexi nodded, then began giggling along with Halley.

Since they often reacted that way when Connor was brought up, I got up off the deck chair I was lounging on and walked to the edge of the pool. Their response to anything I said about him was strange, and at that moment I decided to focus on jumping into the pool to cool off. It was early in the summer, but it was already extremely hot for the second week of June. Diving into the deep end, however, I was at least thankful I didn't have to head to the gym like my friends. The only thing on my schedule all day was swimming and more swimming.

After swimming a few laps in the deep end I climbed back out of the pool and sat down on my deck chair once again. Thankfully my friends had moved on to talking about their upcoming practice by the time I re-joined them. I found it strange in that moment to listen to them. For the first time since I met both of them just under a year ago, I was going to be on a different team than my friends. Sure, being on Fuze had been a little taste of that, but I was still on Blast as well that whole time. It meant a very different season since we were on different practice schedules and wouldn't be performing at the same time during competitions. Not wanting to focus on the separate teams any longer, I brought up something I had been thinking about since I got my new Nitro cheer gear on Saturday.

"Did you guys get sports bras for practice too?" I asked, looking at them sitting on either side of me.

"No," Halley said simply.

"Why?" Lexi asked.

"Well, everyone on Nitro got sports bras with the TNT on the front in glitter letters," I explained. "I wore mine under my tank yesterday, but a lot of people just wore the bra. I wasn't sure if that was what I was supposed to do. I mean, do I have to wear just the bra to the gym from now on?"

"Oh my gosh, you're totally getting good uniforms this year!"

I stared at Lexi after her comment, certain I had missed something. On my other side, Halley was also grinning and nodding in agreement.

"What does that even mean?" I finally demanded.

"We've had the full tops for a few years now," Halley began. "But before that, back when my sister was on Bomb Squad, all the senior teams had half tops. So like the midriff tops we see a lot at competitions."

"That was back when Mario was still coaching," Lexi jumped in. "He did a lot of the uniform designs. But when he left to work at another gym Nicole was put in charge of

77

uniforms. So, we ended up with a simpler look."

"But I guess we have someone new helping out," Halley once again took over. "That means Spark might get a uniform upgrade too. Probably not mid drifts though since Nicole doesn't like them for junior teams. But maybe we can finally get something cool like other teams."

"So, I'm really going to have my stomach showing when I perform?" I asked, trying to make sure I understood all they'd just said.

"Yeah," Lexi nodded. "In fact, you might want to think about getting a new bathing suit. You don't want to blind the judges with your super pale skin."

In that moment, I wanted to tell both of my friends that they were wrong, but I also knew they couldn't be more right if they tried. After all, I never wore midriff shirts or bathing suits like they did. Not even a tankini like Halley was wearing, a term I only knew since the bright pink suit was new so Lexi had complimented her on it when they arrived to my house. Lexi, unlike Halley, was showing a good bit more skin in her yellow and orange striped bikini. The suit didn't look too "grown up" even though it showed her stomach, but the idea of me wearing something like it was strange.

Looking down at my own swimsuit after taking in both of theirs, it was like I stood out like a sore thumb. My hunter green one piece was the only suit I had owned for years, despite the fact I went swimming almost every day. I had no idea how long I had owned it, or even where it came from for that matter. It was something my dad just gave me, having picked it up when he was out getting pool supplies after we moved into the new house. Like so much of my clothing, I just let my dad know I needed something like new socks or basketball shorts, and he would grab them when he was in town. But, I knew instantly, I was going to need some backup on buying something like a swimsuit. Especially one that would actually help me tan my stomach before people would see it while I was performing. Sure, I had a while until then, but as I sat between my friends in their fancy and brightly colored suits, I knew it was time for change.

CHAPTER 9

Despite insisting I needed to go into a store and try on swimsuits, Lexi and Halley helped me order a new bathing suit off line before they left Tuesday afternoon. I knew they would more than likely drag me to the mall at some point for additional swimming options, but when I explained it would be easier on my dad that way, they let it go. There were some things my dad was still a little weirded out about, so I did my best to help him where I could. He was always willing to give me money to buy things, but even mentioning them felt weird. So, instead of telling him what I needed and why and then asking for a ride, I just told him my swimsuit was old and I wanted to order a new one. I picked out a basic suit that would show most of my stomach and allow me to tan, then called it good. I went for a royal blue color in the end since it didn't have any rhinestones or other flashy hardware, unlike every black one I found.

With that taken care of, and another grueling practice Wednesday, I spent the rest of the week trying to get the skin on my stomach to match the rest of my body. I knew it was a bad idea to just sit out under the sun and get it done all in one day. So, instead, I laid out for a little while at a time, taking breaks to swim and cool off from the heat. Although, when Friday rolled around and we were finishing the 3 mile run that was part of our daily workout, I felt like the time tanning might have been a waste. I was feeling sluggish and tired, and worried that a little more time stretching or even going for a run might have been a better idea than trying to get my stomach to be less pale. I finished only a little bit ahead of Matthew, and for once needed to sit for a while to catch my breath.

"Isn't this supposed to get easier after a while?" Connor asked. He was breathing heavily, lying on the blue mat next to me with his shirt off in an attempt to cool down quickly. "Today felt even worse than Wednesday."

"It's because we didn't get a popsicle," Matthew frowned. "And I think it's actually over 100 degrees today."

"103," I confirmed, having seen the temperature while sending Lexi a snapchat just before practice had started. The heat and workout had me tempted to take off my tank top and just wear my sports bra, but I was still hesitant. Cheer shorts took a little while to get comfortable in, and it was looking like the sports bra and crop top uniforms were going to be more of the same.

"So, what do you guys think," Emma asked between sips of water. "Are we actually going to try stunts or tumbling today?"

"I hope so," I replied. "Anything to keep from all the non-stop conditioning."

Despite the wishing, we once again spent the practice doing one hard exercise after another. It was extra grueling considering the girls on both Blast and Dynamite were practicing on the mats next to us. They were working on basic tumbling passes and proper grips for bases. Seeing them out of the corner of my eye while we pushed our bodies through the hard work out wasn't easy to say the least. Thankfully, it came with a bit of good news at the end of practice.

"Okay everyone gather around," TJ called out, while motioning us over to him. We had just done bear crawls across the spring-loaded floor and back five times each. So, we moved slowly as we took a seat in front of our coach who was sitting on a stack of mats. "This week was hard. Now, I'm not going to lie and say the exercises are going to get easier, but they will feel easier, if that makes any sense."

"Not really," someone behind me announced, causing everyone to laugh a little.

"Let me try that again," TJ said with a smile. "Next week we're going to do the same drills. The same warms up, and the same conditioning. Every day for the next three months that's going to be how we get started. And starting Monday we're going to start trying out stunt groups and working on tumbling after everything we just did. But the more we do it, the less tired you're all going to be."

"We're building stamina," Matthew said, many of the athletes around him nodding in agreement.

"Exactly," TJ confirmed. "We're going to push hard from day one, so that when we get to competition time we have the drive to keep going even when it's hot, or we've done a lot of full outs, or everyone around us is tired. So if you want it to get better here, you need to do the work when you're not at the gym as well."

I immediately thought of my time tanning over the last few days. As much as I wanted to work on tanning, I needed to also do conditioning at home as well. Like TJ said, the work at home would help the time at the gym be that much less strenuous. There would likely be a lot more days of exhaustion at practice before things got better, but at the least there was a promise of flying and tumbling soon. I was looking forward to Monday for that if nothing else.

"I also want to talk about something I'm sure you've all noticed," TJ began again, this time with a much more serious look on his face. "This team is a small co-ed. That means we take the floor with 4 guys and 16 girls. That's it. But I'm sure you've all noticed that we have some extra people here. Between now and when we take the mat at our first competition we will be losing 1 guy and 4 girls. Some of the people who get cut will move over to Detonators or Bomb Squad and still have a shot at Worlds. But some of you may get cut and be moved down to Fuze. Either way, people who aren't doing the work at home will not be on this mat a month from now. That's a promise. I can tell when you're just going through the motions or not putting in extra time at home. In fact, I think that's what we did at the end of last season, and it cost us everything."

Beside me, Connor shifted uncomfortable. The mention of Nitro's failure at Worlds was still big and heart breaking news at TNT. Thanks to a pyramid fall that seemed to drain the life out of the whole routine, Nitro walked away from Worlds with nothing to show for it. No trophy. No medals. Just a lot of regrets. Even Connor, who wasn't basing on the side of the pyramid that fell, hadn't brought it up that often in the weeks since it happened. Glancing around the mat, I saw a lot of other athletes looking frustrated or even sad just thinking about it.

"That was last year though people," TJ continued, although it was clear the mention of Worlds had him a little bummed as well. "This is a new team, with new talent. We're going to build a great routine and push from here all the way until that finish line. So when we look back after this year, we can all be proud of giving it all we have. For some of you, even your best will not be good enough for this team. And even if you don't make the final team, you can be proud if you put in the time and actually bring your best each and every time you enter this gym or put on your teal uniform."

TJ finished his speech then handed everyone a half sheet of paper with each step of our workout listed. The idea was for us to use it at home to work on the same skills and drills. After just three days of doing them over and over again, I had a feeling none of us would soon forget the torture. Finally, after circling up for a "Nitro" on three, I dragged myself to the cubbies holding my backpack and sat down to change out of my cheer shoes. They were a little beat up after months of wearing them, but they would get even worse if I didn't trade them for tennis shoes for the trip home. I quickly swapped the pair, then took the chance to also slip on a pair of black basketball shorts over my much smaller teal cheerleading shorts.

"Nice look," Leanne said with a mock smile to me as she also changed out of her shoes. "Real fashion forward."

"Thanks," I replied simply, then turned and walked away from her. I had been tempted to reply with the same level of attitude that she shot at me, but was too tired to say anything more. Not only that, but I was still hoping being on the same team might help her relax with the attitude as far as I was concerned.

"Max, wait up." Stopping to turn around while walking to the door, I saw Connor jogging after me. "Do you want to walk home together again?"

"Lexi and Halley said you live super far away," I said in reply, although I knew it wasn't exactly an answer to his question.

"Yeah kind of," he shrugged, running a hand through his sweaty hair. "But I figured you might like the company."

After thinking about it for only a second I agreed. "Company would be nice. Just don't expect me to go fast after all that conditioning."

"Oh come on," Connor laughed as we exited the gym to grab my bike. "You didn't even look tired until right at the end. Not to mention you're always the first one done with the run."

"The sooner I finish the sooner I don't have to run anymore," I shrugged, giving him the same answer I had told Matthew on Monday.

"Only you would think of it that way Max," he said with a shake of his head. "You're always so positive when the rest of us are dragging."

"Well, right now, I'm positive I'm going to be dragging this whole walk home," I frowned. "If I didn't have my pool waiting for me I think I would die of heat exhaustion or something."

"Don't say that," Connor said with a shake of his head. "You're already killing it at practice, I don't need to be jealous of your pool now too."

"You don't have to be too jealous," I offered. "I haven't planned it yet, but I'm sure I can have people over soon for a swim party after practice."

"Really?" Connor asked, already brightening at the idea.

"Of course! I did it a lot last season with Lexi and Halley and then some of the other girls on Blast. I guess so far this season I've just been too dead after conditioning to think about mentioning it to anyone else."

"Okay, you just made this idea of nonstop conditioning sound a little less terrible," he said with an over exaggerated grin.

"Anything I can do to help, I will!" I assured him. "I'll double check with my dad this weekend, but I'm sure one day next week some people can come over."

"Awesome. Now we just have to survive that long."

With a laugh, we went back to chatting about practice, stunt groups, and Nitro in general. It was so easy to talk to Connor and forget everything else around me. Much like when I was with Lexi or Halley, time passed by quickly and easily when I was with him. In fact, so much so on that day, that before I knew it we had made it to my house.

"Well, this is your stop," Connor said as he put the kickstand of my bike down so it could stand on its own in my driveway.

"Thanks for walking with me, Connor."

"Anytime," he grinned, then moved in to give me a hug. It was a rather gross and sweaty hug after the long team practice not to mention the additional walk through the hot air all the way to my house. Thankfully, it was a shorter hug than usual though. Likely since Connor realized the stifling heat only got worse being that close to people. "See you later."

"See ya," I echoed back, then turned and headed inside to change for a swim. I knew I needed to ask my dad about the pool party, but that could wait. The first thing I needed to do was change into my new swimsuit and jump head first into the pool. And it was exactly what I did.

CHAPTER 10

"I might actually die," I whined Monday afternoon as I laid on the floor after yet another session of conditioning.

Around me, the other athletes on Nitro were also exhausted, panting after our run and workout. It was over 100 degrees outside once again, and even the otter pops TJ gave us as a reward for the miles we completed weren't enough to give us energy. But, like it or not, we still had a lot of practice time to go.

"I'm just focused on the pool," Connor said out loud in reply to my comment, and was instantly given the support of both Matthew and Emma.

Once I got home from practice on Friday I talked to my dad about having Nitro over to swim then set to work inviting people. I didn't know everyone on the team still, but wanted to do my best to invite a few people I knew and use it as a chance to get to a few more people as well. This of course meant I invited Connor, Matthew, and Emma right away. Then, since I was kind of close to her from my time on Fuze, I invited Juleah. From there, I invited Jade and she asked if it was okay if she could bring Nick. They lived on the same street, so he was her ride home. It sounded fine to me, since I hadn't gotten to know Nick that well yet either. I thought about inviting more people, but decided that many was enough for the first swim party of the season.

"Yeah, today's pool time can't come soon enough," I sighed.

Even thinking about the pool had my mind going back to my new bathing suit immediately. I had only worn it a few times since it arrived, but felt self-conscious even when I was swimming alone. I knew if Peter or Kyle had been home and were in the pool with me I would have never put on the bright blue suit that showed off my entire stomach. In fact, even without my neighbors there, I chose to wear my green one piece when I went for a swim to start off my Monday morning. Part of me knew it was kind of silly since no one was even there to see me, but I still felt exposed for some reason. Short shorts were one thing, but a real bikini was, for some reason, a big hurdle for me to jump.

"Hey Max, do you have a minute?"

I sat up at the question, shocked to hear someone other than my friends calling me. Looking over, I saw the question had come from Leanne. She was standing next to Connor, looking as done up as always with a thick coat of makeup on her face, which was somehow unaffected despite the sweat I could see along her hairline. This could have been thanks to the fact that she was one of the girls going without their tank tops for practice.

"Sure," I immediately replied, although it sounded a little like a question. I stood up and walked with her a few feet off the mat.

"So, I was talking to TJ about this season and he is planning some really intense stuff for pyramid," she began, a slightly annoyed sound in her voice. Or rather a more annoyed tone than usual. "The only thing is that he wants to work on some tumbling to lead into everything since it will help the score sheets."

"That sounds great," I nodded, a comment that made Leanne narrow her eyes at me a bit.

"Yeah, great for you," she corrected me instantly. "I don't really tumble much. I'm always doing baskets in the back during the running tumbling. Like, I honestly don't even know the last time I've done more than a whip to layout."

My mind instantly went through Nitro's routine from the season before. Leanne was the point flier, always front and center for any of the skills in the air. But, when I really thought about it, I realized she was right. While the rest of the team did standing jumps and of course tumbling, Leanne did other things. She was thrown into the air for a kick double during jumps and then a super high toe touch during the tumbling. Both moves kept her from doing the same skills as everyone else thanks to choreography before and after both sections. Thinking about it, I wasn't sure if I had even seen her do a layout at all, but tried to remind myself that I had only been on the same squad as her for a few practices.

"Listen," she said with a dramatic sigh and hair flip. "I know we don't really know each other, but we're on the same team now. So I'm coming to you as a teammate to see if you can help me work on my tumbling. Greg isn't free when I have time, so TJ said I should talk to you since you're more or less the best tumbler at the gym."

"Oh," I replied, mad at how lame it sounded. "When did you want to practice?"

"I know we leave here really tired and all, but I'm free right after Nitro practice." She paused as if to wait for me to give her an answer, but then continued when I didn't speak right away. "We don't have to do it three times a week or anything, but maybe once or twice would be good. I just need to be able to do some whips through to full. Or maybe a double full. Or even a kick single. I just need to be a little better so I still look good when I'm point stunt for pyramid."

"That should be fine," I finally said, eliciting a genuine grin from Leanne. I think it was the first one I had ever seen her direct my way. "I can't today, but I think I should be okay to stay after on Wednesday."

"Perfect."

With that she turned and walked away. It was a bit of a shock, but I wasn't too worried about it. For one thing, it was really cool to hear that people thought I was the best at tumbling in the gym. And, on top of that, it was both shocking and kind of exciting that someone like Leanne was coming to me for help. So when TJ finally called us together again and started breaking us into stunt groups, I was instantly happier to get back to work.

"Okay everyone, we're moving on to flying," TJ explained. "We're going to be trying out a lot of groups, so don't get too comfortable with the people you are holding up or the people lifting you."

With that we began a wild hour of trying out stunt groups. We were doing very simply moves, but doing them repeatedly. First, the group we were stunting with would lift us up so we were at their shoulder level, or prep position. Next, they would dip us down a little and lift us as high as they could where their arms were locked out, in a position referred to as extension. From there we would be asked to do a liberty, where we stood on one leg at a time while the other was bent so our foot not being held was right next to stationary legs' knee. Finally, fliers would be brought back down to the ground. Over and over we did this same series of moves, with one group after another.

Just when it felt like we had done the motions a few hundred times with each combination of stunt groups beneath us, we did the same series of skills again, only this time we spun around once on the way from prep level to extension. It instantly caused a few stunts to fall out of the air, and made it a little clearer who was going to be with certain fliers. The move was easy enough for me, but it was hard depending on who was trying to lift me in the air. Time and time again I found myself falling out of the basic move, being caught again and again by the athletes under me.

"What is going on people?" TJ all but yelled. "We're doing single ups! How are we going to get double ups if we can't get this right?"

As if to prove we weren't ready, TJ instructed us to try going from the blue mat up to a standing extension position. This time, however, we did a double around. The change meant I was spun around twice before standing with my hands on my hip to face forward while both feet were being supported by the group of bases under me. It was a move I had mastered just a few months after joining the gym thanks to my extra classes, but was as difficult as TJ had assumed it would be in that moment.

"This would be a lot easier if we weren't so tired," someone on the stunt team next to me mumbled. I think his name was Scott.

"He's going to regret he said that," Connor whispered from his spot standing behind me.

"Why?" I asked, glancing back at him to see a smirk on his face.

"TJ clearly heard him," he explained. "And with an attitude like that, there's no way he's going to stay for long."

Moving my gaze to where Connor was looking, I saw TJ shoot Scott a look then go back to talking to a group on the other side of the mat. Scott didn't seem to notice TJ had heard him, but I knew what was really going on. There were only so many spots on the mat. If someone was already complaining so early in the season, then the spots on Nitro likely wouldn't be filled by that athlete. A part of me felt bad for Scott, but I also was glad for the reminder. I needed to keep a good attitude and keep pushing hard even when I was tired so I could truly earn a spot on the team.

"Gather up everyone," TJ finally called after we tried the double around to extension a few more times. "We're doing easy stuff right now. Super easy. I understand messing up once or twice, but when I give a correction and you don't learn from it I get upset. Today is a throw away day. I'll blame it on the fact that it is Monday or the fact that it's extra hot outside.

Whatever. But Wednesday if I see this kind of mistake after mistake carelessness, then we will go back to even harder conditioning until we start looking like Nitro, and stop looking like my squad was replaced with a bunch of junior level 2 athletes."

As TJ called for a hands in I could tell a lot of people were dejected from his comments. After all, it wasn't really a pep talk. From what I had seen of TJ last season at competitions I knew he was a lot of fun. Everyone who had him for a coach would agree as well. He was a great coach, and a good friend to everyone. But he also wanted people to be perfect. Or at the very least do everything in their power to not make mistakes. People that didn't show that kind of drive tended not to like him much, and not cheer on his squads. I found myself hoping the reaction was from the heat, not a sign of a rough season ahead.

"I want to see Scott and Becca for a second, everyone else is dismissed," TJ said after we had all counted off and yelled a halfhearted "Nitro." I had a sinking feeling that it would be the last time I saw Scott during practices for the teal team.

"You ready to go?" Connor asked me as we began the walk to get our bags and leave the gym.

"So ready," I nodded. Shooting one last glance towards Scott as he followed TJ into the office to chat in private, I was even more thankful for a chance to hang out with my friends and enjoy the pool. There was so much going on at the gym, and the idea of being with my friends outside of the walls of TNT Force sounded like a dream come true. Between things with Scott as well as my interaction with Leanne, I was ready for the distraction of simply swimming and having fun. After all, I knew my time on Nitro might be short lived if I wasn't careful.

CHAPTER 11

"Was this here last time?" Connor asked as we trudged up the final hill on the way to my house. He was clearly just as exhausted as I was, the long Nitro practice taking its toll on us even before the walk to my house. It didn't help that he was also holding my bike up, despite me offering to take it multiple time.

"We're almost to my house," I assured him, although I was struggling myself.

Thankfully, just as I had assured him, we crested the hill and could see the steady decline that lead all the way to my driveway. Setting my bike just inside the open garage then heading inside, we found my dad pulling snacks from the oven. He turned to say hello but was beaten to the punch when Lightning and Thunder began meowing and racing towards us.

"I almost forgot about these two," Connor commented as he dropped to one knee so he could pet the kittens now circling his feet. "They might actually be cuter in person than in the photos you always post."

"Yeah, they're pretty adorable," I nodded. "Definitely worth having to join the gym."

In reply, Connor simply laughed. The news about being bribed with kittens to join the gym was common knowledge. Despite worrying everyone would feel bad when I explained the truth about my new pets, my friends thought it was funny. Likely because it was after Blast and Fuze both won Summit. If I had told people about it all sooner who knows how it could have gone.

"The fur balls beat to me to the punch, but welcome to our house Connor," her dad finally said, walking over to shake my friend's hand.

"Thanks Brian," Connor replied, knowing that if he called my dad "Dr. Turner" he would be instantly corrected. "I would have been over a lot sooner if there was an offer to come over and swim."

"You could have asked," I quickly interjected. "You know Lexi and Halley come over to swim all the time."

"Speaking of the pool, why don't you show Connor where he can get changed," my dad offered.

"Good idea," I agreed. I moved a few feet down the hallway and turned on the light in the bathroom. "You can change in here."

"Thanks," Connor said in reply as he walked into the bathroom, cheer bag in hand.

"So how was practice?" my dad asked as I walked back into the kitchen.

"Long," I said with a sigh. "We were trying out stunt groups so it was a lot of the same thing over and over again. Not to mention it was at least a million degrees inside the gym."

"The weather is supposed to cool down for a few days, so hopefully that will help," he replied before reaching a hand towards me.

He was holding a mini cupcake that I happily took and popped in my mouth after removing the paper as fast as possible. Although the interaction with him only took a few seconds, it was long enough for me to miss my window of opportunity to change into my swimsuit. As I turned to walk down the hallway to my room the doorbell rang. Knowing it was likely more of my friends, I headed to the front door instead of making my dad do the honors.

"You're not in the pool yet?" Michael asked as he entered the house. As soon as I opened the door I saw that him and Emma were both already in their swim suits with their towels in hand.

"No," I frowned. "We had to walk here, remember?"

"Oh yeah," he nodded in reply.

Despite really wanting to go change, at that point I figured I would be the gracious host. So, instead of heading to my room to change, I led them both outside. There was a chorus of hellos to my dad as I led them through the kitchen and then finally onto the back deck. While Michael immediately set his stuff on a deck chair, Emma stood on the deck and stared at the blue water in shock.

"This pool is massive," Emma all but gasped.

"I guess," I shrugged.

Looking at the pool while standing next to Emma, it really didn't seem big to me. Then again, it was always a part of my house, so I was used to it. When I first moved in it might have been considered big to me, but I was just happy to have a way to cool down in the Texas heat, so I never gave it much thought. Whatever the case, even in that moment it was just the same old pool. I knew at one point Kyle or Peter mentioned it was almost as big as the pool at the country club across town, but since I never went there I didn't know how true their statement really was. I also wondered if the fact that the wooden deck went right up to the pool on one side, and the brickwork around the rest of the border made the pool seem even larger than life. Either way, I just shrugged it off as Emma stared in awe.

"Hey Max!" Juleah called out, distracting me as her, Jade, and Nick made their way out of the house and onto the patio. They were being led by Connor who was done changing. Realizing I was the only person not dressed for the pool, I said my hellos then snuck back inside to finally change.

Rushing through the house, I heard someone jump into the water immediately. Knowing it was likely the most refreshing feeling in the world, I tried to change as fast as possible. Thankfully my new swimsuit was easier to slip on than my old green one piece. Once I was changed I took a second to look at myself in the full-length mirror on the back of my door. It made me feel instantly self-conscious that my friends were about to see me with a bare midriff for the first time. Sure, I had managed to even out my tan, but I still felt weird. It was almost like showing my stomach was too grown up for me. Shaking the worries of my head, I walked down the hall, and outside before I could chicken out and put on the old green suit I knew was still somewhere in my laundry hamper.

"Wow Max," Emma gushed as soon as I stepped onto the deck.

"What?" I asked, folding my arms over my stomach to try to cover my pale skin.

"That color looks great on your," she explained. "And, like, how are your abs that defined so early in the season already?"

Glancing around I realized that everyone was looking my way. It made me instantly embarrassed. Sure, Emma had given me a compliment, but I could feel the heat rising in my face. So, I was thankful to be saved when my dad walked out onto the deck with a massive tray of snacks.

"Who's hungry?" he asked.

"Me!" Matthew and Nick both announced, leaving the pool quickly.

Thankful for the distraction I walked over and dove into the pool. I was hungry, but knew that it was a good way to take the focus off myself. The food also helped. But, I was hoping if I swam for a few seconds Emma would move on to something else to talk about. Or at the very least not bring up my suit for a least a little while.

Kicking my legs and stroking with my arms I made it to the far wall of the pool quickly then dove again to swim underwater back towards the ladder closer to the snacks. I wasn't quite ready to get out of the pool, but could feel my stomach starting to groan after the long workout at practice. Dipping my head back into the water to get my hair out of my face, I saw Connor was sitting on the end of the pool, his hair wet from going under at some point. But he wasn't swimming anymore. Instead, he was just sitting and watching me with a hard to read look on his face.

"Are you okay?" I asked, climbing up the ladder and walking to stand next to him.

"Yeah," he said quickly, glancing away from me and instead at everyone a few feet away on the deck. "I'm just so glad we're done at the gym for the day."

Nodding in agreement I moved to grab a plate and load up on snacks. I managed to pile a slice of pizza, a handful of vegetables, and a whole heap of chips onto my plate before finding a seat on a deck chair. Once I

was sitting down I was surprised to see
Connor still sitting in the same spot watching
me. He looked away suddenly when I glanced
his way though. It was a little strange, but I
was too distracted by the act of eating to think
about it too much.

CHAPTER 12

By the time we were done eating all the food we could manage, we did what all cheerleaders in our place would naturally do: we did stunts in the pool. Although Emma was also a flier, it quickly became clear I was much smaller than her which made me easier to throw into the deep end. Now don't get me wrong, Emma is still small by anyone's standards. She often looked even smaller than she was thanks to her extra long wavy brown hair, and light mocha complexion. But, when we were both wearing swim suits it was clear I was a few inches shorter than her and a lot skinnier as well. And in cheer, it made a big difference.

"That was even higher than last time!" Juleah announced after I was launched into the air by the boys high enough to do two backflips before landing in the water feet first. She was standing on the deck taking videos and photos with Jade and Emma, both of whom were calling out suggestions of other moves I should try.

"Okay, let's go with a kick double," Jade called out as I swam back to the boys.

"Boring!" Emma replied. "How about a kick triple?"

I was instantly unsure if I could pull off the move, but was excited to try. Reaching Connor, Matthew, and Nick I hopped up into their arms and waited until we were all ready. Then, with Matthew counting us into the move, I was tossed up into the air. As I finished the revolution of the back flip, I kicked one leg up before beginning the rotations of my body. Two twists were easy enough for me, but adding in another full twist was harder than I first thought. I managed to get my feet in the water first, thankfully, but then got a faceful as well. I only made it through half of the final rotation, something I instantly regretting trying.

"Okay," I coughed once my head was above water. "I think I'm done for a little while."

"You okay?" Connor asked. He reached an arm out to help pull me into the shallow end, then kept one around me while I stood on my tip toes and attempted to catch my breath.

"I'll be okay," I assured him. "No more water though. I think I just swallowed half of the deep end, while the other half went up my nose."

"Alright Emma, your turn," Nick announced as I swam past Connor and climbed out of the pool.

"Not after that," Emma said with a shake of her head. "Max, you have to see that last one though."

Sitting down on the deck chair next to Emma I watched the replay of the last video she took, complete with my face smack on the water. Despite the terrible ending of the video, I thought it looked really cool, especially once Emma played it in slow motion. With my approval, she even uploaded it to her snap story. She also uploaded a few of the ones that had much better endings to both Instagram and Snapchat. It made me feel better about the 'flop' ending, knowing videos showing my well performed tricks were on display for people as well.

"I bet if we tried that kick triple a few more times you could land it," Matthew said after watching the video over Emma's shoulder. "You got a lot of height on that basket for sure."

"Don't say that in front of Leanne," Jade mentioned, leaning back in her deck chair.

"TJ would never take her off baskets during tumbling," Emma assured Jade. "Her tumbling isn't good enough to do anything else during that part of the routine anyways."

"Speaking of her tumbling," I began slowly, not sure if I should share my conversation with Leanne. "She asked me to work with her on tumbling after Nitro practices."

"You're kidding, right?" Nick asked, stopping mid-way in bringing a mini cupcake to his mouth. He looked funny, the small pastry looking even tinier next to his muscled frame, but I managed to keep a straight face.

Shaking my head, I sat up and crossed my legs under me. Connor, who had been standing just a minute before took the chance to sit on my deck chair with me. He sat where my feet had just been resting, and made me realize how close all of us were sitting to one another. That knowledge helped me feel like I could be honest and open about everything without worrying. Even though I was still getting to know Jade, Nick, and in a way even Juleah, I felt like I was really surrounded by friends that I didn't want to keep anything from.

"TJ told her that there's going to be some harder tumbling going into the pyramid," I finally began. "I guess he wanted her to get some more practice in, but she can't go to any of the classes Greg is coaching. So, TJ told her that she would try to work with me."

"I never thought she would ask anyone for help," Emma said honestly. "Leanne thinks she's the best cheerleader in the history of the world. Knowing she actually asked for help is pretty serious."

"Well, she's one of the best fliers we have ever had," Connor said in her defense. "And she's been at the gym basically since birth."

"But she's still human," Matthew added. "It makes me happy to know she's actually willing to get help and admit she isn't the best at something. Her head can get a little too big sometimes if you ask me."

"I was honestly surprised that even with TJ encouraging her she actually decided to talk to me," I said finally. "I'm pretty sure Leanne hates me."

"She doesn't hate you," Nick offered, although I could see a little bit of doubt on his face. "She's just not always welcoming."

"Yeah," Connor agreed. "A lot of people don't get along with her at first. But she's really great once you get to know her. The extra tumbling practice time might be just what you need to finally get to know her. Then she can finally realize how much you two have in common and all that."

"I guess," I shrugged, although I wasn't sure I fully believed the idea.

Thankfully the conversation moved on to chatting about stunt groups, what the new uniforms might look like, and then finally the dreaded topic came up. After Emma mentioned that she might only be flying for some of the routines, Jade brought up the fact that a few people would still be leaving Nitro before the season started. Everyone immediately began guessing who would be cut from the team, although it was hard for us to agree since practice earlier in the day had been so rough.

"Do you think Scott will get cut?" Emma asked after we decided there were too many girls getting cut to even stress about it for the time being.

"It's either him or me," Nick said with a shrug, eliciting a chorus of protests. "Seriously though. We're the new guys, so it's going to be one of us moving to Detonators."

"Unless they make a big move and send one of us to Detonators instead,"

Matthew commented, although everyone knew it was the farthest thing from the truth.

It was common knowledge at the gym that athletes only moved around on the level 5 teams if they either requested the move, or were asked well before assessments. It was rare, and since Connor, Matthew, or Aaron hadn't talked to TJ about making the move, the chances of Nick leaving Nitro were sadly just as high as his chances of staying. It didn't help that Nick was the shortest of the guys on the team, which could be a downside for things like partner stunts or pyramid. He was still strong enough to lift any of the fliers, but with the guys all so even on other things, anything could be a deciding factor. Thinking so much about Nick, I suddenly realized there was a real possibility that I could lose my spot on Nitro as well. It would be easy for me to be moved down to Fuze, or even for Juleah to head back to our squad from last year's team. As new members of Nitro, we were just a few of the girls who were basically on the chopping block.

"So, what happens if I was moved to Fuze?" I asked, feeling nervous even mentioning it.

"That won't happen," Emma assured me quickly.

"Exactly," Jade agreed. "You're basically the best flier on the team. Just, again, don't mention it to Leanne."

"Yeah" Matthew added. "You've got nothing to worry about."

"Alright, no more talk about cheerleading," I decided, feeling the weight of team cuts more than ever.

My change in topic worked for a little bit, but in the end, we continued talking about the gym. I tried to fight it at first, but then realized how lucky I was. Not only did I have friends over that I could have fun and hang out with, they were also people who understood the whole part of my life that was dedicated to cheer. Of course, Lexi and Halley were also there for me when it came to things at the TNT Force gym, but Peter and Kyle never fully got it. They went to competitions and would even ask me about cheer stuff, but they could never sit and have a conversation with me the way other cheerleaders could. So, sitting with my fellow athletes from Nitro around my pool just chatting and joking about drama at the gym, it was strange to think I'd ever even considered leaving the gym after my dad's two week bribe was up.

CHAPTER 13

"If you're not going to stay in the air then you're not going to fly this season," TJ yelled on Wednesday, speaking over the sound of his hands clapping the beats of the skills we were performing. "Again, from the top."

I took a deep breath, pushed sweaty strands of hair off my face, then lifted my foot up to prepare to be picked up once again. I was in a stunt group with Juleah, Scott, and Jade and was just barely managing to stay in the air each time we tried the single around to heel stretch. It was a simple enough move, but my stunt group was not doing as well as they could. A few of the other groups were struggling as well, but all of TJ's attention was on the two groups that were consistently falling. One group was Emma's and the other was stunting a flier named Lilly. It was clear everyone was tired after all of the conditioning. Not to mention that the weather was even hotter than earlier in the week, despite the initial forecast predicting a cold front moving in.

As my group lifted me into the air I did my best to keep my body straight and tight. Despite my friends assurances that I had a solid spot on the team, I didn't want to assume anything and get lazy. Using my arms for extra momentum, I twisted them with my body and planted my left fist on my hip before kicking my right leg up and holding onto my foot for a heel stretch. My grip on my foot was strong, but under me I could tell something was shifting. One of the hands on my shoe wasn't where it needed to be. As the grip was adjusted to make up for the initial error, I knew I was going to fall.

The fall lasted only seconds, taking me from standing over 5 feet up off the ground to pitching sideways towards the mat. But, the entire thing seemed to happen in slow motion. As I fell all I could think about was turning my body so I would land on my side or back instead of face first into the blue floor beneath me. Squeezing my eyes shut and bracing myself for impact I felt the wind knocked out of me as I finally landed. I tried to take in a breath, but instead only heard a wheezing noise as my chest again constricted. Trying once more, I could feel at least some air being inhaled, which was an instant comfort.

"Give them some room," a voice said, although it was hard to hear with the gasps and other comments being made.

It wasn't until I heard that comment that I realized I was not on the blue mat. Instead, of hitting the mat directly, I had landed on someone. Rolling onto my side as I tried to catch my breath, I opened my eyes and saw it was Juleah who had broken my fall. In the process of landing on the ground, I made contact with her face at some point, causing a massive nosebleed.

"We need ice," TJ called out before helping Juleah sit up. "Max, how are you doing sweetie?"

I tried to speak but couldn't. I simply wasn't taking in enough air just yet. Instead I coughed a few times then decided to lay flat on my back in hopes of it helping somehow. Closing my eyes at the bright gym lights I willed myself to take a few deep breaths, focusing on the sound of my breathing to help my body calm down. Putting all of my energy into taking long and slow breaths made me unaware of what was going on around me. So, when a familiar voice spoke next to my ear, I was surprised to realize it was Tonya who had moments before been quite a distance across the gym.

"Does anything hurt Max?"

"I don't know," I managed, opening my eyes to look at her. "I got the wind knocked out of me."

"Yeah, I saw that," she nodded. "How's everything other than your breathing?"

"My head kind of hurts," I replied after thinking it over. "But I think it's just from falling. Like, my whole body feels sore, but not really hurt."

"Do you think you can try to sit up?" she asked.

Rather than answer, I decided to sit up immediately. It was not the best idea, since I felt dizzy right away. Bending my legs, I rested my feet flat on the mat so I could rest my arms and then my head on my knees. Closing my eyes once again, I tried to be patient until my brain stopped spinning. Once I was certain the spinning feeling had passed, I lifted my head, opened my eyes, then gave Tonya a reassuring smile.

"I'm okay," I said simply. "How's Juleah?"

"TJ just walked her into the office, but I think she's doing okay," Tonya explained. "Why don't we head that way as well. If your head is hurting we need to make sure it's not a concussion or anything even more serious."

I wanted to protest, but knew if I my dad was at the gym he would have already been by my side running through his concussion checklist. During a soccer game once I slipped on wet grass and went down right as someone was kicking the ball. After taking a foot to the head, my dad made absolutely sure I wasn't suffering from a concussion before he even let me go back to practice, let alone an actual game.

Standing up with the help of Tonya and a few athletes around me, I made it to the office without having any trouble. My head was no longer dizzy and my body was sore but overall fine. In fact, when I walked into the room and saw Juleah sitting on the ever-present medical table in the corner of the room, my only concern was for her. She just looked so miserable, her red hair and pale skin only seeming to draw attention to the smudges of blood on her face and hands. On top of that, her bright blue eyes were even more intense when rimmed with red from crying.

"Are you okay?" I asked, then continued without waiting for a reply. "I'm so sorry Juleah. I didn't mean to hurt you."

"I'll be okay," she said, her voice muffled by the ice pack pressed to her face. "But don't worry about it. Catching you is my job, remember? Besides, if I wasn't standing under you, you could have gotten really hurt. My nose will be fine. It doesn't even feel broken."

Despite assuring Tonya and TJ I was okay, I sat next to Juleah as they checked my vision. They also asked me questions to see if I was at all confused or disoriented, and then finally called my dad to let him know what happened. TNT Force took head injuries seriously, so I tried to be patient. Eventually TJ went back into the gym while Tonya stayed with Juleah and myself. I wasn't sure what TJ was saying to Nitro, or rather my stunt team, but what I could overhear sounded rather loud and angry. It made me feel a little bad, but then again, I knew that as minor as our injuries were, it could have been a lot worse.

"I'm not bleeding anymore," Juleah said once Tonya had finished calling both of our parents.

"Can we go back to practice?" I asked instantly.

"Max," Tonya said with a bit of a laugh. "You just took a big fall. Don't you want to rest for a little while?"

"Not really," I shrugged. "I know my head is okay. I mean, you checked and don't think it's a concussion. So, I might as well get out there and practice again. Competition season will be here before we know it."

Tonya tried to argue with me, but it was only done halfheartedly. It was clear to her that I was going to head back to practice, no matter what anyone had to say. Juleah joined me, and we got back to our squad just as they were finishing up some extra conditioning exercises. Apparently, TJ decided that it was a good way to spend the time until the team found out if we were both okay.

"How are you feeling ladies?" TJ asked us, looking extremely concerned despite his happy tone.

"Great," I said with a smile.

"Less great, but still pretty good," Juleah said next to me. She had a red and purple bruise on her nose and there was a good chance she would end up with a black eye as well. But, nothing was broken so that was one thing to celebrate.

"We're going to spend a little time on choreography since Tonya is here," TJ then explained to both of us. Part of me was a little bummed we weren't doing more flying, but I knew it was also the best idea after my fall. "I hope everyone is ready to dance."

Dance was my least favorite area of cheer, since I struggled with it the most. But Tonya was a great choreographer and was sure to give us a dance section that was both high energy as well as entertaining for anyone watching. I knew all of the Worlds teams at TNT also had an additional choreographer that came in later in the summer and then again closer to the actual start of competition season. In the meantime, however, Tonya was there to get us started. When she instructed us to line up to get started though, I was caught up in a hug before I even knew who was next to me.

"I'm glad you're okay," Connor said in my ear while giving me an extra tight squeeze. "Hopefully I get to be in your stunt group from now on so I can make sure that doesn't happen again."

"Hopefully," I nodded. Then, as I stepped back from the hug I realized something. "Scott's not here anymore."

"Nope," Connor nodded. "TJ was super mad he messed up his grip and dropped you. Then when TJ mentioned it, Scott blamed you for not holding your weight or shifting funny or something. Basically, TJ got super mad and told him to leave. I don't know if he's off Nitro for good, but TJ was so upset when you and Juleah hit the mat I have a feeling Scott will be trying for a spot on Detonators after this."

I was in shock, but didn't have time to reply. Tonya was instructing us in the first part of the dance, and was calling me over to join a group of girls on the left side of the mat. Following her instructions, I tried not to think about Scott leaving. After all, it got us one step closer to the final Nitro team for the season, and hopefully also one step closer to having a team that could win Worlds. As terrible as the thought might have been, I knew it was the reality of Nitro. Especially since the real goal wasn't just to get down to 20 people. We also needed to get down to 20 people who could finally bring home a Worlds championship to the TNT Force gym.

CHAPTER 14

"Need a walking buddy today?" Connor asked as practice finally ended. Despite assuring everyone I was okay, it was clear Connor and a few others were still keeping a close eye on me.

"Not right now," I said with the shake of my head. "I'm working with Leanne today."

"Oh," he replied with a concerned look on his face. "Are you sure that's a good idea?"

"I'll be okay, promise," I assured him, then walked over to grab my water and find Leanne.

The day before she had sent me a direct message on Snapchat to figure out details. Once I told her I was free on Wednesday and Friday, she suggested we start with Wednesday and go from there. Her replies to me were always short and straight to the point. It gave me the feeling she was not looking forward to the practice time together, but I tried to remind myself what everyone else had said. Leanne wasn't big on asking for help, so the fact that she even reached out to me was progress in a lot of ways.

"You ready?" I asked her before taking a long drink of my water.

"Sure," she said slowly. "I assumed since you got hurt we wouldn't work together today."

"I'm fine." Saying it yet again made me feel like a broken record. "I'll be over by the running track when you're ready."

Not wanting to hear anyone else make comments about my injury, ask me how I was doing, or suggest I not stay to do more tumbling, I walked over to the corner of the gym where the foam pit and trampoline tracks were located. I set my glittery teal backpack in an open cubby and sat down to stretch. My body was feeling a little stiff from the fall, but other than that I was feeling fine. Thankfully I also had ice packs and hot pads I could use at home if any part of my body was still feeling sore later in the day.

While I was stretching, I used the time to check the various notifications on my phone.

I was excited to see that Tonya had already uploaded a few videos of the dance routine we had just worked on to the gym's Instagram account. A few videos showed mistakes, often made on my part. But, it was cool to see the progress that led to a final perfect run. TJ also posted a few videos to Instagram and even Snapchat, since he was always filming practice. He usually only did so leading into Worlds, but so far had a camera set up for every Nitro workout all season. I had a feeling my fall was even on video, not that I was quite ready to relive that moment.

"Mind if I join you?" Connor asked, sitting down next to me before I could give him an answer.

"Are you staying?" I asked. Glancing over my shoulder I saw his black backpack in the cubby next to mine.

"If that's okay," he said in reply. "I just figured it would be a good chance to practice tumbling. Not to mention I can make sure you don't go too hard and hurt yourself or anything."

Rolling my eyes at Connor, I was going to tell him that I didn't need him to stay. But then I remembered our time practicing with Greg during our skills class all winter. Working on tumbling passes and even standing tumbling was easy enough to do on my own. But Connor was always great to have on hand to encourage and even push me. So, I quickly changed my mind, accepting his offer. Sure, the main reason I was staying was to help Leanne, but I also knew it would be a good time for me to work on my skills as well.

"Ready to get started?" Leanne asked while walking towards me with a less than happy look on her face. She seemed to brighten when she saw Connor was sitting with me as well, but only by a little. I had the feeling she wasn't thrilled about putting in more work after the long practice.

"Let's do this," I nodded in reply to Leanne's question, standing up and quickly setting my phone with my backpack. "We should warm up for a little, I'm thinking. That way I can also see what skills you have and how we can get them to the next level."

"Sure," Leanne said quickly, then walked over to the long and skinny trampoline.

Taking a few running steps, Leanne easily performed a round off back handspring before ending in a back tuck. I watched the series of skills, trying to see any weak points. It was clear that she wasn't getting much height on the tuck to end the pass. She repeated the move a few times, occasionally keeping her legs straight, turning the back tuck into a layout. Each time it was clear she wasn't getting high enough off the trampoline to do additional moves like a full. The rotation during the backflip required more time, and that was only achieved with a bigger bounce going into the motion. Not to mention she was sure to get even less height on a spring-loaded floor as opposed to the trampoline track.

"Are you just going to watch the whole time?" Leanne asked after performing the same tumbling pass yet again.

"No, I'm just thinking," I explained. "I think you need to bend you knees a little more after the back handspring and really push off with your arms more."

I could tell she was a little confused, so I stepped onto the track and showed her what I meant. It was hard for me to end the tumbling pass in a layout, since I was used to finally doing fulls. On Blast and Fuze I was limited to only back tucks or layouts, so being on Nitro and getting to end with a full was beyond exciting. Going back to not throwing them, however, was an instant downgrade in my mind for sure.

After I showed Leanne twice she tried again. Bending her legs worked some, but I could tell she didn't really have the strength behind the move to get enough height. So, it was back to the drawing boards. First, we tried to add in another back handspring to help her get height, and then a whip before the final layout. Both helped some, so I decided it was time to try something harder.

"Let's work on your full for a little bit," I suggested, walking to an extra long air mat that led to a large pool like area filled with foam blocks.

Over the next hour, I went over the twisting motions of a full with Leanne time and time again. I could tell she was struggling with them, mostly because she wasn't getting her body to twist around fast enough. The foam helped though, since if she under rotated she was still landing softly and safely. Even with the foam to land on, however, I could tell she was getting frustrated.

"Why don't we stop for now and pick it up next week," I finally decided right after Leanne failed at doing even a back tuck. It was the first time I had ever seen her make a mistake of that level, so I knew she must have been exhausted. She basically just did a back hand spring and then flew backwards, unable to get her body going into the next motion. That kind of an error was referred to as 'balking' in the cheer world, and I could tell Leanne was upset the second it happened.

"This sucks," she muttered, clearly upset at herself.

"You did really great up until that last one," I assured her. "It takes time to learn something like a full."

"How long did it take you?" she asked.

"Max has leg strength from other sports," Connor interjected. "And she's shorter than you, so it's a little easier for her. It took me a whole month to get my full."

I was thankful Connor was there more than ever in that moment. If Leanne knew that the first time I was at the gym I almost landed a standing full, she likely would have had some not so nice things to say to me. Instead, she thanked Connor for his comment, as if he has been the one helping her the whole time. While in reality, he was sitting and filming or taking pictures while we worked so we could show Leanne her progress or how she needed to change her body position. It proved to be a big help, even if she didn't manage the full by the end of our time practicing.

"I'm sure you'll get it next week," I encouraged. "Or if you want to work again on Friday I can stay after again. And I'll be at the open gym."

"I'll let you know." Leanne moved to stand close enough to Connor that her arm at her side was all but touching his hand as well. "Want to walk out with me?"

"Not today," he replied with a shake of his head. "I'm going to do some tumbling while I'm here. I got lots of rest while you were practicing so I figure I might as well work on some things."

"Okay," she said slowly. "Text me later?"

"Sure," he nodded, then turned back to face me. "You staying, right Max?"

"Absolutely."

Only half aware of Leanne making a frustrated noise before turning and walking out of the gym, I headed to the air mat. Despite already making it through a full Nitro practice and the extra tumbling work, the idea of practicing my kick double suddenly gave me lots of energy.

CHAPTER 15

I was more than thankful that Connor asked me to stay and work with him. As much as I wanted to, I didn't get to work much while I was helping Leanne. Sure, I got to do a full here and there to show her how it should look, but it was nothing compared to what I was able to work on once she was gone. Time and time again I was able to race down the air mat and launch my body into the air. Progress was a little slower than usual, but before I knew it I was getting the height I needed for the skill I was hoping to achieve.

"Ready for the kick double?" Connor asked after I had done a few double fulls and kick fulls.

"I think so. But just on here. I don't think I can land it on the floor yet."

"Not this week at least," he joked, before taking off to throw a pass of his own.

I took a deep breath, then decided to try the move Connor had suggested. I was on the air mat, which was better than the spring-loaded floor but also not as helpful as the trampolines. It would give me a good understanding of whether I was actually ready to try the skill on the blue cheer floors. After building up some speed and height I went for it, kicking my leg up before snapping it back down before spinning my body hard to the left. Once I finished the second twist, I planted my feet on the ground, and only had to take two small steps forward. It wasn't a perfect landing, but was the best I had done so far.

"Told you," Connor laughed. Ignoring him, I took a long breath then turned so I could try again running in the direction I had just come from.

I continued like this for a while, trying the kick double over and over until I was getting enough height on it to almost spin my body around another half of a twist after the kick. After every try I was aware of Connor glancing my way, clapping, or even commenting on how good I was doing. I paid attention to all of this only slightly. The rest of my focus was on building my confidence to try the double full on the less helpful spring loaded floor. It was still more of a boost than normal ground, but would make everything a little harder. Feeling like it was a "now or never" moment, I grabbed a sip of my water before heading to the open cheer floor closest to the foam pit to give everything a try for real.

"You can do this," Connor called out, taking a seat at the edge of the mat to watch. He again had his phone out, and I knew he was likely filming me once again.

I wish I could say that I ran, threw all the skills including the kick double, and landed perfectly on my feet. Instead, I did my usual font punch, round off, followed by a back handspring and a whit. Then, I attempted the kick double, landing on my feet only to pitch forward onto my knees. It wasn't even as good of an attempt as when I tried it at the assessments to kick off the new cheer season. But, it simply fueled me to go again. And again. And again. Connor eventually gave up filming, although he still sat to watch and encourage me the whole time. I stayed determined through all the attempts, but none of them was landed on my feet without falling or taking steps off the mat, at the very least. A few of the attempt also ended me sitting on my bottom or bouncing my knees hard onto the blue floor beneath me.

"Okay, I'm done," I finally frowned after once again falling backwards to sit on the mat, despite only trying a simpler kick single.

"Ready for me to walk you home?" I opened my mouth to protest Connor but he continued. "If I don't walk with you, I have a feeling TJ will make you call your dad. Even after all your flips I'm sure he's still worried about you biking home alone after that fall earlier."

"You're probably right," I said with a sigh. "I really feel fine though."

"I'm sure you are," he nodded. "But it was a super nasty fall. I was surprised one of you didn't break something."

"Well, not for lack of trying," I laughed. "If I hit her face any harder, I have a feeling I would've broken Juleah's nose."

Connor agreed, explaining that it was pretty scary to watch. He was across the mat when it happened, and was upset knowing he couldn't do anything to stop it. Apparently, a few of the bases that were closer to me tried to help. But in the end, no one could help me but Juleah. Sadly, her attempt caused her face to be nice and bruised, and still left me feeling pretty shaken up overall. The one thing that helped was reminding myself that it really could have been so much worse. Just last season a flier on Fuze took a tumble and broke her collarbone. It allowed me to join the team for Summit, but meant an end to that athlete's time cheerleading for the time being. There was no word if or when she could return to the gym, something that would crush me despite my initial hesitation to join a cheer team at all.

"Max!" voices screamed from across the room, freezing both Connor and myself in our places.

We had just grabbed our bags and began walking through the gym. Flame was practicing on the mat closest to the gym door, and there was a group of super tiny girls learning the basics like somersaults and the ever important "cheer face" on the next mat over. Thankfully outbursts like the one that made Connor and I pause was rather common in the gym. So much so that no one else seemed affected by it all.

"Hi," I managed in reply before I was all but tackled by Halley and Lexi who had raced towards me immediately after calling my name.

"Are you okay?" Halley asked.

"Why didn't you go home?" Lexi also asked at the same time.

"Nice to see you guys too," Connor joked.

"Let's go outside," I suggested, letting out a laugh as both girls began to apologize to Connor.

"Okay, tell us everything," Lexi demanded as soon as we made it outside. "You're okay, right?"

"How did you even know I got hurt?" I asked in reply, still confused as to why they were at the gym.

"Juleah posted a selfie on Instagram," Lexi explained.

"And then Connor posted a snap that you were working on tumbling despite your 'really bad fall' earlier," Halley continued. "That's how we figured you were here and not at home."

"So I asked Matthew about it, and he agreed to drive us to the gym," Lexi finished, then pointed to where Matthew was sitting in his Jeep across the parking lot.

"They were freaking out," he called out to us with a bit of a shrug.

"I'm fine, really," I told them yet again. "Juleah got hurt way more than I did, and even she was okay."

"Well, since were here we might as well give you a ride home." I wasn't sure if Lexi had checked with Matthew before she offered, but since he was still sitting in his car waiting I assumed it was an idea they all came up with together. "And we can give you a ride too if you want Connor."

"Sure," he agreed, then began removing my bike from the wrack where it was waiting.

"We also may or may not have brought our swim suit so we could hang out in the pool at your house too," Halley explained as we walked towards the waiting car.

"Perfect," I smiled, then turned to Connor. "If you want to swim too I know we have extra swim trunks in our laundry room."

"Or we can stop by your house," Matthew call out, having heard the conversation.

"Either way works for me," Connor shrugged. "As long as we get out of the heat soon."

I nodded, climbing into the back seat with Lexi and Halley as Connor climbed into the passenger seat after loading my bike into the back. We debated the options for a little, and in the end decided to stop and get Connor's suit before heading towards my house. It also allowed us to stop and get ice cream at the Dairy Queen down the street. As we pulled out of the drive through I text my dad that a few people were coming over and he of course asked about my head. That gave me the warning that I was due for a long checkup once I walked through the front door.

"You haven't felt dizzy or nauseous at all?" he asked both after shining a penlight into my eyes and making me follow his finger from side to side without turning my head.

"Nope," I replied. I was a little annoyed, but also knew my dad was just worried about me. "I did extra tumbling after practice and just felt a little sore overall. But I think that's partly because of how long practice was today."

"If you start to feel anything, even a headache-"

"I'll let you know right away," I finished, cutting him off. "Promise."

For a second it looked like my dad was going to press the issue but then he simply gave me a hug, a kiss on the forehead, and went back to slicing fruit. He had a variety of snacks started when we got to my house, most of them were much more healthy than usual. This was more than likely an attempt to put things good for me into my body to counteract any damage caused by my fall. Whatever the real reason though, we were all thankful for a bite to eat, followed by a long and relaxing time in the pool. I didn't swim as much as usual, since the long day at the gym was catching up to me and I was starting to feel tired. Well, that and I also kept seeing my dad peeking out the back patio door make sure I wasn't suddenly struck dead or something equally as dramatic.

"So, did you ever land your kick double on the mats?" Lexi asked as we all sat on deck chairs after finally getting out of the water.

"How did you know that's what I was working on?" I asked in reply, only partly because I didn't want to admit my failure at landing the skill.

"Connor's snaps," Halley said simply.

"You posted my tumbling?" I turned to face Connor who was sitting on the other side of me talking to Matthew about a zombie show they both watched.

"Yeah," he slowly replied. "Didn't they already say they saw my posts earlier, and that was how they knew we were at the gym?"

"Maybe," I answered, my voice not so sure. "I guess I didn't know you took videos of me and posted them."

"I can delete them if you want," Connor quickly offered, searching on the table next to him for his phone.

"No, it's okay," I said, reaching out to take his phone. "As long as they don't look too terrible."

With both Connor and Lexi watching over my shoulder I flipped through the videos that were on Snapchat, and the few that were still only on Connor's phone. All in all, I was pretty pleased with what I saw. Although I never landed solidly on my feet, my form for the kick double looked good. From the look of things, I just needed a little more height. Eventually, my muscles would be so used to the skill I would be able to do it in the sleep. Much like how easy it was for me to do back handsprings and even a standing full.

Handing Connor his phone back finally, I leaned back in my deck chair and smiled. "I'm landing that kick double at the open gym Saturday. Mark my words."

CHAPTER 16

The day by the pool with my friends was great, but left me exhausted. Between the fall, the extra tumbling practice, and then hours of laying in the sun, I was ready for bed nice and early. I almost felt bad for not inviting Lexi and Halley to stay the night, but I knew I wouldn't be much fun at a sleepover. They understood, especially since we were planning a girls' night at Lexi's house on Friday so we could all go together to the open gym the following morning.

Knowing I was going to need all the practice I could get to land my kick double, I spent Thursday working out just as hard as if I was at a Nitro practice. I swam laps, went for a run around the neighborhood, and then did a long core workout. This included a lot of time balancing on a homemade stunting stand doing flying poses and a lot of squats to get my legs ready to really push off for the height I needed. The extra workout was exhausting, but made me feel even more confident about my skills at Friday's practice. However, when I walked in the gym doors I immediately noticed someone was missing.

"Is Scott really gone for good?" I asked Matthew and Emma after we were done with our 3 mile run. Until then I assumed he was late and would be entering the gym at any moment. But, as more time went by, I began to realize he wasn't going to be there.

"You didn't hear?" Emma asked, looking both shocked and kind of sad. When I shook my head, she continued. "TJ told him he was going to be an alternate since his skills weren't quite there for Nitro or Detonators, so he left the gym. He's trying to get into a few different gyms in Dallas, so hopefully he will still get to cheer this year."

"Oh," I managed, feeling instantly terrible.

"It's not your fault, Max," Mathew assured me, wrapping one arm around me. "He didn't quite have the tumbling skills yet, and he hasn't been basing that long either. Out of all the guys he was the one that we all kind of knew was going to be leaving the team anyways. It's just a bummer it took you and Juleah getting hurt before it became official."

I nodded, but couldn't shake the thought that if I had worked a little harder in the air then I might not have fallen, and he still would be on the team. From the second I knew someone's grip on my foot was wrong, I should have said something. I should have stopped my flying post and told my team to bring me back down. Then I might have given all of us a better shot at succeeding at the stunt, and kept myself and Juleah from getting hurt. I knew blaming myself and dwelling on it wasn't a good idea since we still had a lot of Nitro practice ahead of us for the day, so I tried to shake it off and just focus on practicing for the time being.

After our usual conditioning, we once again worked on our stunts. We did about single and double arounds to both prep and extension level, but then began working on harder moves while we rotated stunt groups as needed. There were a few fliers that worked with the same people repeatedly, but I noticed that myself, Leanne, and Mary were trading groups after almost event stunt. I thought it was a little strange since we were all the lightest girls and any stunt group would have no problem keeping us in the air, but tried to only focus on doing my best on each skill. We stuck with doing a double around on the way up into the stunt, then TJ had us try heel stretches, scorpions, and even needles before either cradling down or even trying a kick single down. It all left me tired, but also extremely happy when TJ told me the good new at the end of practice.

"Okay we're going to leave Max with Juleah, Matthew, and Addison," TJ said before turning to the rest of the athletes on the mat. "Leanne and Mary, let's try something a little different."

I could tell that Leanne was a little bummed, since she had been on a stunt team with Matthew and Addison the year before, but I was too excited to think about it much. Not only was I in a stunt group with two of my best friends on the team, I could already tell Addison was a great base and I was excited to get to know her through the season. Although last season was only her first time trying to base after years of flying, she clearly had been putting in a lot of extra time and was giving each stunt her all at every run through. All in all, I was super happy for the season knowing I had a great team under me for our elite stunts and baskets.

"We should do a stunt group bonding time," Juleah suggested as the four of us sat on the mat waiting for our next instructions from TJ. He was still talking to Leanne and Andy's groups, and running a few stunts with them.

"Pool party at Max's house?" Matthew asked with a big grin.

"Of course!" I laughed. "Maybe we could have a Nitro team party or something."

"You mean like all of Nitro?" Addison asked. "That's kind of a lot of people."

"Why not?" I shrugged. "I know my dad would be happy to have everyone over. He told me yesterday he loves when I have friends over to our house since it gives him the chance to cook all kind of new things and play in the kitchen. I think he misses when him and my mom used to have big dinner parties with their friends in Oregon."

"Well, just let me know the time and I'll be there," Addison noted.

While the other groups worked with TJ, it allowed my new stunt group a chance to chat. That, in turn, also gave me a chance to continue to get to know Addison. She was really skinny, but was pretty tall. In fact, she was one of the tallest girls on the team. Thanks to her recent growth spurt that started half way through the cheer season before last, she went from flying on Bomb Squad to being a base for Nitro. She loved Nitro though, and even when we were working hard and it was super hot inside the gym she had a big grin on her face. In fact, she even had teal bands put on her braces so once we began competitions she would match her uniform. Addison's braces were the second thing you noticed when you first saw her though, thanks to her long grey hair. It had once been rainbow colors, and hot pink at some stage as well, but now it was a silver gray that looked great against her tan skin and grey blue eyes.

After a few minutes sitting and chatting with my stunt team, TJ called everyone to their places. He wanted to see how everything looked with the stunt teams he had just changed, and try a little bit of what would later become our elite stunting section. We all stood up and were waiting for our next instructions when TJ made the announcement I never saw coming.

"Alright Max, I need your team to trade spots with Leanne's team."

"What?" I heard someone near me ask, but was too confused to figure out who it came from.

"But that's center," I reminded TJ, as if he didn't know.

TJ simply nodded, then waved his hand to indicate we needed to make the trade. As I finally turned and began moving from my spot a bit back and just right of center, I saw Leanne and her stunt group move as well. The look on Leanne's face was confused and almost hurt, but she still walked to the new place on the blue mat. She had been on the center, or point stunt, for two years, always being the flier representing the team the most prominently. But suddenly, I was given the position while she was basically demoted' to a less featured spot. I had seen the drama it had caused when a similar thing happened on Detonators the year before, but being a part of it made it worse. It was bad enough to know that Scott was no longer on the team after he made a mistake while in my stunt group, but then to know I was also the cause for Leanne not being on point stunt was a lot to take in all at once. So much so that when practice was finally over, I raced straight over to talk to Leanne.

"I'm really sorry," I said immediately. "Maybe it's not TJ's final decision."

"No worries," she assured me with an even smile. It was a side of Leanne I was certain I would never have seen even a few months prior. "It makes sense really. You're super tiny so your group can throw you really high and pull some good stunts. You'll look best right in the center. Just enjoy it while you can."

"I'll try. I just feel bad," I explained.

"We're all on the same team here Max," Leanne went on. "As long as we make it to Worlds and finally take home those rings, I'll be happy."

I wanted to believe her, but Leanne still looked a little defeated despite the smile on her face. "Do you have time to work on tumbling for a little bit today?"

"No," she said with a shake of her head. "But I'll be at the open gym tomorrow."

I wanted to apologize again, but before I could, Connor ran over and gave me a massive hug, picking me up off the ground and spinning me around. Despite still feeling bad about taking Leanne's spot on the floor, Connor's hug had me beaming.

"Center stunt? Are you kidding me?"

"Yeah, it's pretty great," I laughed, trying to regain my balance once he set me down. When I turned to look at Leanne she was already gone, now standing near her cubby looking at her phone.

"First this, and tomorrow you're going to land your kick double," Connor quickly reminded me. "You know, if you weren't my best friend I would be mad at you for making the rest of us look bad."

"Speak for yourself," Matthew said walking over and making a show of flexing his arms above his head. "I look amazing."

With a laugh, I walked with Connor to get my things. I was getting a ride home with Matthew because of the sleepover I was having with Lexi. Despite this though, Connor carried my cheer bag for me to the car before giving me another hug goodbye. It was common enough, but also a little odd. I assumed it was simply him showing me how excited he was for me to be placed on point stunt.

"I'm really glad we're on the same squad this year," he told me after the embrace.

"Me too," I grinned. "Last season was awesome, but I'm already getting excited for Worlds."

"Between your tumbling and having you on point stunt I think this might finally be our year," Connor said. "See you guys tomorrow."

I echoed his goodbye as I closed my door. Then, I began to buckle up as Matthew started the car and let out a laugh as Connor finally walked away.

"What?" I asked him, certain I had missed something.

"You still don't get it, do you?"

"Get what?" I asked, even more confused.

"Nothing," he replied putting on his sunglasses. "You're just too adorable Max."

Although his comments were confusing, I shrugged them off as I waved at Connor out of my window. He waved back then walked into the gym. As he did, I noticed Leanne was exiting the gym, looking pretty upset. I tried to give her a wave as well, but she was focused on her phone, her fingers typing furiously. Knowing she was likely more upset about being taking off center stunt than she let on, I made the mental note to work with her a lot at the open gym. If she wasn't on point flyer anymore, I was determined to help her get her tumbling to a higher level. Hopefully it would help soften the blow of the position change, as well as make me feel a little less guilty.

CHAPTER 17

"How do you guys manage to do this?" I asked Lexi and Halley as we sat in Lexi's bedroom later that night. We were all sitting on the floor painting our nails for the open gym. I had protested at first, but then decided it might be time I learn how to do my own nails for a change. It would be helpful come competition season, not to mention it was easier than trying to reason with my friends. Sure, I could head to the salon with Tonya closer to Worlds like we had done going into Summit, but that wasn't something we could do before every competition all season.

"Just go really slow, and make smooth and even stokes," Halley explained, although it was mostly hopeless. Painting my left hand was pretty much impossible since I was a lefty. It ended up looking like I just stuck my fingers in the bottle. "Here, I'll help you with this hand."

I felt a little bad for still needing help, but was pretty proud of how good my right hand looked. I only got a few spots of color on my skin, and the uneven brush strokes could be covered with glitter. Lexi had given me that piece of advice and I was thankful that months of cheer made me okay with the idea of putting glitter on my nails. After wearing glittery makeup, uniforms, and cheer bows, my whole bedroom seemed to have a constant light dusting of glitter. So, having a little more on my nails didn't really seem like a big deal.

"Are you wearing your Nitro practice wear tomorrow?" Lexi asked as Halley finished fixing my left hand.

"I think so," I shrugged. "But, I brought a few options just in case."

"What if we all wore our matching Summit shirts from last season?" Halley suggested. "I have mine in my bag."

"I don't have mine though," I said with a frown. "But maybe we can match bows?"

Blowing on my nails to help them dry faster, I watched as Halley grabbed her overnight bag to see what bows were attached. There were quite a few that I remembered her buying during competitions last season, as well as a lot with the familiar TNT Force logo on them. Moving to compare her bows with the ones I had on my backpack, I watched as her face suddenly lit up.

"We can wear our neon best friends forever bows!"

At Hallie's suggestion Lexi jumped up and raced to her closet. She came back holding black chevron tank tops that perfectly matched the bows. Clearly her obsession with the pattern the season before was a good thing. There was a pink one for Lexi, a green one for Halley and a blue one for me, each matching the colors of our bows. Lexi handed them out to each of us, although she was careful to keep our freshly painted nails from getting smudged in the process.

"I might need to wear another tank under this one," Halley commented, holding the tank up to her body.

She was only a little taller than Lexi and I, but she was not as thin as us. The tank top looked like it would work, but it would be a bit of a tight fit. Halley wasn't fazed by it though, and immediately opened her bag to look for something to wear as a layer under the green tank. Holding up a black thin strap tank top she proudly announced that the plan was a go.

"What shorts should we wear?" I asked, going over the options I had in my bag. "I have the black ones from tryouts, my teal pair, and then my red shorts from Fuze."

"Black for sure," Lexi nodded, then walked back into her closet to find her matching pair.

With our matching outfits figured out I happily began adding the glitter coat to my nails. Halley come to my rescue to on my left hand, applying a shimmery silver glitter over my teal nails. I realized a different shade of blue would have matched the bow better, but it was a small thing. I knew the polish would only stay on for a few days with the amount of time I was in the pool. Not to mention as soon as it started to chip a little I couldn't help but pick the rest off immediately.

"Do you want your phone?" Lexi asked me, picking it up from its spot on her bed. "You have a lot of missed notifications."

"Sure." I took my phone, careful to not mess up my nails. Unlocking my phone with my fingerprint I was shocked to see I had well over 300 missed notifications on Instagram. "What the heck?"

"What's wrong?" Halley asked as both her and Lexi moved closer to me.

"I'm not sure," I said honestly as I began to scroll through my notifications to see what happened since I last checked my phone.

The first few dozens of notifications were all announcing people who were now following me. I was used to getting a few here and there, but never anything like that unless it was right after a big competition. I had a lot of new followers and activity after winning Summit, for instance. But, as I scrolled down further I saw that people were mentioning me in comments, saying things like: "You'll get it next time" and: "So close, keep trying!" There were so many of the comments that it was hard to keep track of them. Finally, I was able to make it down far enough to see that everything seemed to stem from one post. Or rather one video.

Clicking on the image, I watched a video of me trying the kick double on the blue mat earlier in the week. It was one of the videos Connor had filmed and then uploaded to social media. Watching it, it was clear that the video showed one of my worst attempts. In the short clip, I landed on my feet then pitched forward, taking two steps then falling first to my knees and then also smacking my hands on the ground as well. My face was close to also hitting the ground, but thankfully I stopped myself in time.

The confusing thing about the video was that people were not commenting on it thanks to a video posted on Connor's page. Instead the video was posted by a handful of different cheerleading accounts. One was dedicated to cheer fails, and another few were just cheer updates. They had all simply posted the video, but it was another account each time that tagged me in a comment, letting anyone seeing the photo know who it was they were watching fail at the skill. The account that tagged me every time was one called Cheer_Spotlight_TX.

"Have you heard of this account before?" I asked to my friends who were watching in shock over my shoulder.

"That one yeah," Halley said. "They've shared some of the photos the gyms' account has posted. I don't know all of the other accounts though."

"I follow that one I think," Lexi added, pointing over my shoulder at one account's name. "They do uniform reveals a lot in the fall."

"I don't get it," I said, my brow furrowed in thought. "Someone took the video Connor posted and put it up on their pages too?

"Looks like it," Lexi nodded, a frown also on her face.

"Connor's account isn't private," Halley reminded us. "Anyone can access what he posts. Someone must have seen it and reposted it. In fact, a lot of other accounts might have also posted it and you're just not tagged in it yet. Who knows how many more people put this up on their page besides these ones."

Staring at my phone I was a little worried, but then I saw that the accounts all had a lot of posts of other cheerleaders also falling. The posts were often the same across accounts, either because someone sent everyone the videos, or they were shared content. The one thing I noticed that really made me happy though, was that not many people were saying mean or negative things. Sure, I fell in the video, but they were being extra encouraging and supportive. It made me feel a little better about the whole situation.

"It's kind of cool," I finally said. "Sure, a lot of people saw the video of me fall. But, after tomorrow they can see a video of me finally landing the kick double."

"That's a good way to look at it," Lexi replied, although she didn't look convinced.

"But I still don't think I would want a video like that of me all over Instagram."

As Hallie agreed I saw even more notifications popping up on my phone. The new people following me were watching tumbling videos I posted, liking photos, and commenting all over the place. In just a few hours I went from having less than 400 followers to well over 1,000. Not to mention the people following me were actually checking out all my different posts. It was a little weird to wrap my head around, so when my phone rang and I saw it was Connor calling, I was happy for the distraction.

"Hello?" I asked, surprised that Connor was choosing to call me instead of just send a text or snap.

"I'm so sorry Max!" He said quickly. It was clear he was talking about what I had just seen myself.

With a laugh, Lexi went back to setting out her outfit for the open gym and Halley added a glitter coat of polish to her nails. I, on the other hand, had to tell Connor over and over again that I wasn't mad at him, that everything was okay, and that there was no need to be sorry. Sure, it wasn't really my plan to have all this attention suddenly, but it was still kind of cool to see people so interested in all my posts about cheerleading. One of the videos I posted of Blast's pyramid sequence during Summit was getting a lot of attention. People were even commenting how funny it was to hear my dad singing along to the team's music while filming.

"So, you're really not mad?" Connor asked one final time, at least 10 minutes into our conversation.

"I'm really not mad," I said yet again. "It's just fueling me even more to land the kick double tomorrow. Hopefully people will see a good post of me actually landing a skill."

"I'll make sure I'm filming, and upload it right away," he offered, and I made a mental not to make sure he followed through on that promise.

CHAPTER 18

After the strange discovery of everything on Instagram, I was happy that the rest of the night was much more relaxing. My phone was still buzzing pretty often as more people continued to follow me and go through my posts. I usually only posted to my account once or twice a week, but made sure to upload some videos from recent practices, photos from last season, and a good 'slumber party photo' after Lexi's suggestion. In total, it was less than a dozen photos added to my account by the time we reached the gym, where Connor was waiting for me. Wrapping me in a big hug he apologized a few more times, clearly still feeling bad for all the craziness that his post had suddenly caused.

"Don't worry about it," I told him again after returning the extra long hug. "If I was mad I would let you know. But it's actually kind of cool. I mentioned in a post this morning that I'm going to try to finally land the kick double today and people have been writing good luck and all kinds of stuff!"

"You're turning into the cheerlebrity and the season hasn't even started," Connor laughed, finally letting me go so he could walk with me to check in at the office.

"A cheerlebrity?" I echoed.

"Yeah," he nodded. "You know, a celebrity cheerleader."

"I know what it means," I said quickly. "I just don't think anyone cares about me."

"Trust me, people care," Connor finally said, an unreadable smile on his face.

The facial expression was confusing, but I was distracted with signing my name on the open gym clipboard sitting on a table outside of the gym offices. Once we all wrote down our names and signed the page, I parted ways with Lexi and Halley. Since Halley was on Lexi's stunt team, they were using the open gym time to work on their skills. Callie and Whitney, the other members of their group were waiting on one of the blue mats, stretching and working on their standing jumps. Lexi was more than likely going to be the point stunt this coming season for Spark, so they wanted to make sure they spent as much extra time working on things as possible. After all, being point stunt was a big honor and responsibility. Something I was still trying to wrap my head around myself.

Knowing my focus was on the kick double, Connor walked with me to the trampoline track to get started. I was also planning to work with Leanne, but I didn't see her when I first walked into the gym. Hoping to find her later, I went to work throwing the kick double with the help of the trampoline. It was pretty easy to work into after only a few kick singles and similar moves. After landing it a few times on the trampoline I headed to the air mat for more work.

Much like at the assessment just a few weeks prior, I was planning to do a punch front, round off, back handspring, and whip all leading to the final kick double. I wanted to add in another whip to help get height, but that felt like cheating. If I wasn't allowed to do it on the competition mat, then I wasn't going to try it just to land the kick double for the first time. Instead I just did the same pass over and over so my body would begin to get used to it and build up my muscle memory. Even when I thought I had enough height I tried to push harder and harder with my arms and legs so I knew I would still be okay once I made the move to the real mat.

"Should I record this one?" Connor asked, watching me as I landed the third kick double in a row.

"If you want to," I said between sucking in deep breaths of air. "But it doesn't really count if it's not on the spring floor."

"Only you Max," he laughed. He handed me my water bottle which was sitting next to him. Once I took a long drink of water and handed it back to him he continued. "Ready for the mat?"

"I think so," I nodded, then wordlessly walked to the blue spring loaded floor closest to me.

I was the only one on the mat, so I quickly did a more basic pass to help my legs gets used to the floor. Then, I stood in the corner and did the pass part by part. I started with just the punch front. Next I did the punch front but added in the round off. I did this over and over again, each time adding in the next skill in the tumbling pass. Once I had the rest of the pass good to go I ended it first with a back tuck. Then, I tried it again landing it in a layout, followed by another pass ending in a full. From there I worked in the kick single, and finally a double full. In that moment, I knew the only skill left was the one I had been working on for weeks: the kick double.

Slowly walking back to the corner of the mat where I started each tumbling pass, I took long breaths to ensure I was ready for what was next. I could feel the nervous excitement building in me, but paused to close my eyes and just calm down for a few seconds. Then, once I knew I couldn't delay any longer, I open my eyes and focused on the far end of the mat. I knew exactly where I needed to land if everything went as planned. So, before I could convince myself to try a safer pass or chicken out completely, I took off, running three strong steps before launching into the punch front.

As my body flipped through the air, it felt like time seemed to slow down. Seconds turned to minutes as I was aware of each and every twist and turn my body was making. I pushed with my legs and arms harder than ever before, feeling my body flying higher and higher off the mat below me. Every move was getting me closer to the moment of truth. The moment when I needed to finally throw the kick double.

With my body flipping in a long straight line after the whip I felt my feet hit the ground and pushed off as hard as I could. Then, as my body flew up into the air I kicked my right leg high before bringing it down to begin the first of two full rotations. I was spinning fast enough and knew I was high enough in the air. I just needed to get my feet under me. Finishing the final of the two twists, all while my body also completed the flipping motion it was making, I bent my knees and reached my feet down to find the floor. Both feet managed to make contact with the mat at the same time, my legs bending to cushion the landing. I held my breath then, squeezing all my muscles and willing myself not to pitch forward or fall to either side. I popped up off the mat slightly, something that was common even for moves like back tucks. Finally, after what felt like a full minute I straightened my body to stand fully upright, my feet firmly planted on the ground.

Before I could stop myself, I gasped then looked towards where Connor was standing and filming me. Only it wasn't just Connor standing there. Instead, Connor stood with Halley, Lexi, TJ, Gwen, Matthew, Emma and a handful of athletes I didn't know by name. As the realization of what I had just done sunk in for everyone, the crowd of people came racing towards me, jumping and giving me hugs. I had done it. I landed my kick double on the spring-loaded floor for the first time ever.

"It was perfect!" Matthew cheered, picking me up as countless arms wrapped around me from different directions.

"Did you get it on film?" I asked, my question directed at Connor who was standing just outside of the mass of people celebrating.

"Yup!" he grinned. "Come see."

Reaching Connor took longer than usual, since a lot of people wanted to give me a hug or high five along the way. But, eventually I made it to him and give him a big hug before grabbing his phone to watch the video. Connor wrapped one arm around my shoulders and watched with me as I pushed play. The video showed me from my first step leading into the punch front all the way to the moment I gasped then turned to look towards where my friends were watching.

"I just did that," I said a little in shock. "I did it."

"Why don't you do it again and prove it wasn't a fluke," TJ challenged from where he stood watching me with a massive grin on his face.

Opening my mouth to protest, I was both excited and mortified as Greg quickly clapped the series of claps that regulars at the gym were used to hearing. As the athletes around the room repeating the rhythm of the clapping then got quiet, I realized what was going on. I was going to have every person in the gym watching me as I tried to kick double for a second time.

"Gather around if you have a second people," Greg called out once the room was silent. "Max just landed her first kick double full and wants to show everyone how it's done!"

I knew something like that should scare me. I knew that I should be intimidated as athlete after athlete walked over to the mat where I was working and found a seat to watch. I knew I should have cringed as a bunch of people also pulled out their phones to snap a photo or take a video of the attempt. I knew all of it should have made me nervous. But instead, it fueled me with even more confidence.

Standing on the corner of the mat once again, I looked around at everyone watching. For a second I thought I saw Leanne in the crowd, but it was hard to be sure since so many people had gathered. Enough people, in fact, that when I finally took off across the mat and landed the entire pass perfectly once again, the gym was all but deafening as the sounds of cheering and celebrating rang out. This was partly thanks to the sounds echoing off the tall steel walls, but my focus was mostly on the celebrating in that moment.

"That was even better than the last one," Greg assured me, after I was once again hugged and congratulated by athlete after athlete. "Now we get to start working on your Arabian."

"How about next week?" I suggested, still in shock that I landed the kick double not just once but twice.

"Deal," he agreed, then turned and began to herd the other athletes off the mat. "Okay people, back to work."

As everyone finally trickled away I had a chance to catch my breath, get some water, and finally sit for a little while. I was joined by Lexi, Halley, and Connor who were still brimming over with excitement for my accomplishment.

"Are you going to post the video?" Lexi asked Connor.

"Sure," he replied. "Or I can send it to Max and she can post it."

I instantly nodded in agreement. "I want to post it first. But feel free to post it after that or whatever."

With a nod, Connor immediately went to work sending the image to my phone. It gave me a chance to look around the room for a second before turning to my friends with a question, "Was Leanne here?"

"Yup," Halley said immediately. "She was over here watching your final pass with everyone."

"So, where is she now?" I asked simply.

"She left," Connor answered, although I hadn't realized he'd been listening to our conversation. "Right after you landed the kick double I saw her walking out."

That fact confused me, but I got a little distracted as Connor handed me my phone as the video arrived in a message. After watching it through one more time, I uploaded it to Instagram. My phone began buzzing due to notifications right away. People were already giving the video views, likes, and comments congratulating me on landing the kick double. Taking it all in I couldn't help but smile. Although it looked like I wasn't going to get to work on tumbling with Leanne at all, I landed my kick double finally and even managed to get it on film not once but twice. All in all, it made for a pretty great morning.

CHAPTER 19

After landing the kick double, the rest of the open gym time seemed rather mundane. I did a little bit of tumbling for fun and then decided to work with Matthew on partner stunts. We knew we would likely be together for our partner stunts, since we were together for our elite stunts and baskets. Once I was ready for a rest after a long while of stunting, I spent some time watching Lexi and Halley work on their flying with their stunt team. It made the afternoon much more relaxing after the initial excitement and work that went into landing my complete tumbling pass.

The rest of the weekend went by quickly as I helped my dad around the house with cleaning and even some yard work. Well, that is after we went out to dinner Saturday night to celebrate my new skill. My dad was so happy when I showed him the video that he actually called the gym to thank the staff for helping and encouraging me. Not to mention for also pushing me to accomplish such a lofty goal time and again, or at least that was how he put it on the phone. I had a feeling it was just the beginning of the thank yous, especially when I saw he was looking up local stores that sold those fancy fruit bouquets.

"Here's our star tumbler," Matthew called out to me as I walked into the gym Monday afternoon for practice.

"Very funny," I said dryly, although I couldn't help but smile at the same time.

Taking a seat next to Emma and Juleah after putting my bag and bike helmet in a cubby, I was hoping to avoid any more talk about Saturday. Unfortunately, I didn't luck out on that one. Instead, both girls began telling me about the posts they had seen on Instagram. At least two of the cheerleading accounts that posted my fail video also posted the success video Connor filmed for me. It had more follows, likes, and comments, all of which was becoming a little overwhelming.

"You're turning into a cheerlebrity," Emma grinned at me finally.

"What?" I asked, remembering Connor suggested the same thing just days before.

"Seriously?" Leanne asked, taking a seat next to us as well. "You don't know what a cheerlebrity is?" She started explaining the term, complete with examples, of well-known cheerlebrities before I could stop her. "Basically they're the girls everyone wants to be and the guys everyone wants to date. Not to mention they get all kinds of free stuff just for posting photos to their social media accounts."

"I know what it is," I said once she was done. "I just don't think I'm anywhere near that level."

"Oh," Leanne said which was followed by a rather awkward pause. "Congrats on the kick double."

"Thanks," I replied, a little shocked considering she looked genuinely happy for me. "Do you want to work on your full again today after practice?"

"Not today," she said holding up her hands that featured perfectly manicured nails. "I have a nail appointment today. I need to get them redone since they're growing out. But I can on Wednesday."

"I'm going camping Wednesday night," I explained. "We're leaving right after practice and then won't be home until Friday morning just before practice."

"Camping?" Juleah asked, looking horrified. "Like real camping? In the woods? With tents and stuff?"

"Of course," I began eagerly. "We go to the same place every year with my neighbors. They meet us on their drive back from California and we go fishing and hiking and everything. There's not much cell phone service, but it's still really awesome."

In reply, all three girls just stared at me. It was like they were waiting for me to say, "Just kidding," and start telling a different story about how we were actually going to go stay in a fancy hotel somewhere and live off 5-star room service meals and hang out with rich and famous actors. Okay, maybe not quite something on that level, but they were clearly not impressed at the idea of sleeping in a tent in the middle of the trees.

"I'm free tomorrow if you want to meet here or even at my house," I said to Leanne, knowing that talking about camping would get me nowhere. "My dad ordered me an air mat so I can work on tumbling at home. It should be there when I get home tonight so I can set it up and test it out and everything."

"What?" all three girls asked at once, catching the attention of a few more athletes nearby.

"Everything okay?" Jade asked, sitting down to join our conversation.

"Max's dad bought her an air mat to use at home," Emma explained quickly.

"Wait, like a real one?" Jade now had a look on her face that was somewhere between shock and awe.

"I guess," I shrugged, feeling suddenly self-conscious. "He was really proud of me landing my kick double and wanted to get me something to celebrate."

"Those things cost, like, over a thousand dollars," Leanne quickly noted, causing my jaw to all but drop open. "There are gyms that don't even own them since they are so much more expensive than trampoline tracks."

I managed a halfhearted "Oh," before I was interrupted by TJ who called out that it was time for Nitro to begin our running. The 3 miles were sure to be pretty easy since the weather was finally cooling down, but still had most of the athletes around me groaning. I, on the other hand, was happy for the distraction. Hearing how much my dad might have spent on the mat was a little shocking, although I knew we were fortunate enough to have enough money for things like that. After all, my dad has a great job at a cancer research clinic, so I guess I often didn't think about things like how much we spend on different items most other families had to really budget to afford.

Thankfully the run took my mind off the air mat, and gave me something to focus on instead. And the focus, as always, was finishing my miles before Matthew. He was getting faster and faster, but I was determined to still finish first. That meant pushing myself harder than usual, but it paid off. Or rather it paid off during the three miles. After I finished the last few minutes of the run, in a pace much faster than my usual speed, I arrived at the gym and instantly regretted my choice. Mostly because it left me much more exhausted during conditioning than usual.

"Max, are you doing okay?" TJ called out as we were doing bear crawls from one side of the mat to the other. "You're looking a little green."

"Maybe," I replied, although it wasn't a very good answer to his question or even his statement for that matter.

"Trash can's over there," he reminded me, then went back to yelling at people who were moving too slow or trying to cut corners on the bear crawl drill.

I never thought I would be pushed to the point of puking during conditioning, but clearly it wasn't an impossible situation. This was proven true as I ran off the mat and quickly emptied my stomach into the can TJ had just pointed out. Thankfully I had Gatorade in my cheer bag so I was able to refuel quickly and get back on the mat. TJ checked if I was okay quickly, then encouraged me to keep working. It was how he treated anyone who threw up during practice, so I was expecting it. Not to mention, sitting out on any of the flying practice was not even close to an option for me.

"Don't puke on me, okay?" Matthew asked as we were finally lining up for partner stunts. As expected, I was paired with him once again.

"I should be fine now," I promised. "Next time I might have to let you win during the run."

"I'll believe it when I see it," he laughed, then turned to ask Liz a question.

Liz was assigned to our partner stunt group to serve as a spotter. She was a new member of Nitro, after moving up from Dynamite last season. I was still just getting to know her, since she was rather quiet. It was odd to find someone at the gym who didn't have an outgoing personality, but Liz proved that for some people, being a cheerleader didn't mean you had to fit into a mold. She had poker straight black hair that drew even more attention to her dark skin and perfect complexion. But, when she wasn't on the cheer mat she wore thick glasses, large gold hoop earrings, and always had her face in a book. In fact, she often was reading while stretching before practice, getting in a few more chapters while she had the chance.

"Alright everyone, we're doing some basics to start, so everyone better stay in the air," TJ began after he assigned everyone to their groups. "I just want to see a simple walk in to start. Every group needs to do 20 of those then we can move on to working on doing toss to hands 20 times and then toss to hands with a press extension 20 times as well."

I couldn't help but exchange a big grin with Matthew, since all of the skills TJ wanted us to start with were going to be extremely easy. Not only because I was so small and Matthew was so strong, but also because we had done much harder skills together during our stunt class all winter. But, knowing that the harder moves would come later, we began with the simple ones that had been assigned to us. First, I stepped into Matthews cradling hands while he lifted me up to shoulder level and turned me to face forward. After 20 reps of that, he held my waist and lifted me up to either shoulder level, or up all the way to the full height of his reach, or extension level. Each time I bent my knees and pushed off the ground as hard as I could so it would be even easier for him to lift me into place. It allowed us to progress through the reps quickly.

"Are you serious?" Liz asked as Matthew set me on the ground after the final toss to hands press to extension. "That was like flawless."

"We've worked on partner stunts before," I explained with a shrug, then looked around to see how the other groups were doing. Most of them were still working on the toss to hands, with only Leanne's group on the toss to hands with extension. But, as I was looking around I noticed some people were missing. I was still learning who everyone was, although we were still required to wear our bows with our names rhinestoned onto them, which helped. Even still, there were some people I never had the chance to talk to. So, as I looked around and couldn't figure out who was missing, I simply started counting. We started the season with 25 on the team, but after Scott left that should have left us at 24. I counted twice to make sure, but was still only counting 22 athletes on the mat.

"Who's gone?" I asked Liz and Matthew, interrupting a conversation about grips for other basing skills.

"What?" Liz asked, before Matthew could reply.

"Amber moved down to Fuze and Hannah R is on Bomb Squad now," Matthew explained. "They were both on Spark last year, so they're still pretty excited about team placements."

"How did I miss that?" I asked. Beside me Liz seemed unaffected by the news, likely meaning she had noticed well before I did that people were gone.

"Well, you might have seen it sooner if you hadn't spent part of conditioning bringing up lunch," Matthew paused. "Literally."

Rolling my eyes, I made a mental note to really get to know the people on the team I hadn't talked to much. Even on a team of just 22 it was hard to spend a lot of time chatting when we were running, conditioning, and working hard whenever we were together. Sure, I knew all the guys by name, and every girl's name was on their bow. But I wanted to do more. I knew if I was moved off the team I would want people to realize I was gone. Knowing that, I could only assume everyone else felt the same way.

"We should have a team cookout and pool party at my house," I said out loud. Although it was the second time I mentioned it, I was much more serious than the first time I brought it up to my elite stunt group.

"Tonight?" Matthew asked.

"No, maybe this Saturday?" I thought about it a little longer then added, "Or Sunday even. I just feel like now that we almost have the team finalized I want to make sure I'm getting to know everyone better. I mean, we're going to be together all season."

"That's a great idea," Liz nodded. "Count me in."

"Me too," Matthew nodded.

"Great," I smiled. "Three people down, 17 more to go!"

CHAPTER 20

After a chat with my dad to figure out details, we decided Sunday would be the perfect day for the party. It was sure to give us enough time to get the house and backyard cleaned and decorated, even with the camping trip coming up. Well, the decorating was an idea from Emma, who came over along with Matthew, Connor, and Jade to swim after Monday's practice. We decided we would start the party at 11 so everyone could swim for a little while before lunch was ready. Then we could of course stay for a while after lunch to eat and swim and hang out.

Since Emma was the one who decided we needed to get teal table cloths, balloons, and more, I insisted she go with me to the party store in town to get supplies. Jade helped look while the guys walked around trying on costume items or sword fighting when we weren't looking. Despite their distraction, we filled a whole corner of the basement with bags of everything teal they sold at the store and then some. The non-teal items consisted of lots of white, black, and silver glittery decorations to go with all of the teal.

The party planning had me super distracted, so I didn't get to try out my air mat until Tuesday morning, just an hour before Leanne was coming over. It was still weird to think Leanne was going to be at my house. Not that I didn't want her at my house, I just wasn't quite sure she would agree to meet outside of the gym. But in the end, after a little while of sending messages back and forth, we decided that she would come over to work in my backyard. Feeling like working right next to the pool would make us want to swim, I let her know to also bring her swim suit.

I spent the early part of the morning getting the air mat inflated and ready to go. Then, I got it all set up in the grass at the back of my yard that was shaded by a long row of oak trees. With it finally ready for use, I worked on my own tumbling for a while. After Greg mentioned learning to do an Arabian, I looked it up online and tried it out. After working so hard on double fulls and kick doubles, it was pretty easy for me to get used to twisting my body around in the air for the Arabian. I wasn't sure if I had it exactly right, but it was feeling close to perfect when someone calling my name startled me.

"Max?" the voice said again, and I instantly realized it was Leanne.

"Over here!" I called, turning and jogging to where she was standing behind the fence gate.

Clicking the latch and swinging the gate open, I was only a little shocked at the amount of bright pink and other neon colors Leanne was wearing. She had on a sports bra and matching cheer shorts that were covered in a crazy splattered and swirled pattern all in bright oranges, greens, pinks, and yellows. It seemed to bring out her tan, blond hair, thick makeup, and massive lime green cheer bow even more. I suddenly felt silly in my usual Nitro tank top and shorts. Not to mention I wasn't even wearing a bow.

"I rang the doorbell twice, then decided to just try walking around," Leanne said while I paused to assess her outfit. "I'm just glad I found you."

There was an awkward pause, and in that moment, I felt like inviting her over without Lexi or Halley or even Connor there as a buffer there was a terrible idea. But, then I just dove right in instead, "The mats are over here."

"Your house is really big," Leanne commented as she walked across the grass behind me. "And when you said you had a pool I didn't know you meant a pool like that!"

"Oh yeah," I replied. "I was really happy when we moved here and found this house."

"Why did you guys choose to live in Wichita Falls?" Leanne asked. "I mean, why not Dallas?"

"My dad's research lab is pretty close," I explained. "Only 20 minutes from here. So, it was perfect. We get to be near his work, and we also didn't have to be too close to Dallas. My dad doesn't like big cities."

"Interesting," she said in reply, then set her glittery teal backpack down in the grass. "Should we get started?"

"Sure," I agreed, thankful for the suggestion.

It was kind of weird to start our time working together, but things got better quickly as Leanne made a lot of progress. Apparently being out of the gym helped her focus a little more, and in no time at all she was landing the full at the end of a tumbling pass with only a small step or two afterwards. I knew it was as good as it would get until we had a spring-loaded floor to try it on as well, so we decided to take a break and enjoy the pool. I swam around in the deep end for a bit, while Leanne went in the water up to her neck and then floated on one of our seldom used inner tubes.

"Do you ever wear makeup Max?" Leanne asked after she explained that she didn't want to mess her face up when I asked why she wasn't swimming. She also explained that she needed to be ready to impress, since her brother was in town and had cute friends over.

"Not really," I replied to her question honestly. "Lexi and Halley try to make me wear makeup outside of competitions every now and then, but I always fight it."

"Why?" Leanne asked, her face looking more like a sneer than anything else.

"I just don't like it," I said simply. "Growing up I never played with makeup. My dad doesn't really know much about it, and my mom was gone before I was old enough for her to teach me anything." I paused to think about it. "A lot of the girly stuff is still really foreign to me. It's why I didn't want to do cheer at first. But I'm glad I finally gave it a try. I still don't really enjoy all the glitter and sparkles and all that, but if it means I get to do skills like kick doubles, then it's worth it."

"I guess that makes sense," she replied, then gave me a long look. "Why don't you wear the Nitro sports bra at practices?"

I was thrown off by her question but recovered quickly. "It just makes me feel really exposed. It was hard enough to get used to wearing the super small practice shorts, so I can't imagine having my whole stomach showing too."

"But you have abs," Leanne pointed out, with a bit of a frown. "And the uniforms this year are going to be a crop top style and you'll have to wear them for competition. Why not get used to it now?"

"I haven't really thought about that," I said, slowly making my way to the pool ladder. "Okay, I'm getting hungry. Do you want anything?"

"What do you have?"

"I'll bring out some options," I offered, then climbed out of the pool and walked inside.

It felt nice to get out of the sun for a minute, not to mention it was also nice to get away from Leanne's critical eye. Despite the fact that we were having a good conversation, it was still kind of weird being around her. I tried to tell myself that it was a good first step, spending time with her outside of the gym and all. But it still wasn't as easy as I wanted it to be. I knew it might have been a little easier if more people were there, but that would have to wait for Sunday.

"Okay, I found some chips, pretzels, leftover potato salad and then some strawberries," I announced listing off the items I had found. I had brought it all with me, just barely managing to carry everything. Thankfully, there was plenty of room on the patio table next to our towels for me to set everything down finally.

"Great," Leanne said standing up from the deck chair she was sitting in and moving to grab a few chips.

Popping a large strawberry into my mouth I walked over to grab my phone, looking under my cheer shorts where I was certain I had set it. When I didn't see it there I glanced around and saw it was sitting on the small end table next to Leanne's sunglasses and phone. Although I didn't remember leaving it there, I was too distracted by a text from Emma about even more decorations she thought we should make. I replied, letting her know the ideas were great, as long as she was willing to help create everything. Then I returned to the patio table to get more to eat. Between the tumbling and the swimming I was hungry to say the least.

CHAPTER 21

"You really did it?" Kyle asked, all but jumping up and down. "You really landed the kick double?"

"Yeah, it's on video!" I assured him, pulling out my phone from the pocket of my basketball shorts. "When we get home, I can show you on my new air mat too."

Moving closer to look over my shoulder, both Kyle and Peter watched the tumbling pass with me, cheering right along with everyone in the video. I had seen the footage a lot by that point, both in showing it to others and thanks to activity on Instagram. It was shared a good number of times on different cheer accounts, and people still commented and liked the original post I made pretty often. No new notifications were coming through anymore though, since the campground didn't have any cell service. In fact, knowing how little I would use it over the two night trip, I didn't even bother bringing my portable charger to keep the battery alive for even the trip home.

"Oh, and I did an Arabian today before practice too." I quickly pulled up that video while I had both of my friends right next to me still watching. "Lenny met with me to work on it for a while since I couldn't stay with TJ or Greg after Nitro practice was done."

"Are you wearing a bathing suit?" Kyle asked in shock.

"No," I replied quickly. "It's a sports…. outfit."

"You mean a bra?"

"Uh, yes," I said then quickly continued. Talking with Kyle about things like bras was just too weird. "Our uniforms are going to be a crop top style this year so I have that to wear during practice so we can get used to it."

"That move was really cool," Peter finally spoke up, coming to my rescue.

Peter reached out and pushed play again on the video, distracting Kyle in the process. I was more than thankful, since the sports bra still wasn't something I was totally on board with. After my conversation with Leanne though, I decided trying the sports bra at practice would be a good idea. It was a little weird feeling so exposed, especially after seeing the look on everyone's face when I first took off my tank top. But, by the end of the practice I was more okay with it all. I only hoped that by the time the competition season rolled around I would be 100% comfortable.

"That was really cool," Kyle finally said giving me a high five and everything. "Even if you were wearing just a bra."

"Sports bra," Peter and I both corrected him at the same time.

"Okay, who's ready for some fishing?" my dad asked walking up to us. He was carrying a tackle box and some rods while Mr. Morgan stood next to him with a cooler that I knew likely contained both snacks and worms to be used as bait. "Dinner won't catch itself."

The fishing trip down to the pond and back kicked off the camping trip perfectly. We returned with enough trout for dinner and breakfast, which gave us lots of energy for a full day of hiking on Thursday. It kept me moving and active, which was nice since I was kind of missing my normal cheer workout routine. I knew that I was still getting good exercise in thanks to the hikes, but it still felt weird to not go for a run and do my now standard core workout. But, at the end of the night as I sat around the fire I realized just how tired I was. Clearly the activity all day was enough to give me a good workout, not to mention it didn't give me much time to catch up with Peter. So, sitting by the fire we finally had the chance to really talk about all that had happened since I was placed on Nitro.

"Isn't the point stunt that Lea's girls spot?" Peter asked after I went over a little of what had been going on at the gym while he was in California.

"Leanne," I corrected him, even though he had gotten it almost correct. "Yeah. it was her spot but TJ moved me there instead. I guess since I'm easier to toss and lift and everything. I've been doing harder stretches lately too, so I'm getting a lot more flexible. Maybe not more flexible than Leanne, but better than last season for sure."

"So how are things going with Leanne overall? She's the one that didn't like you last year, right?" Peter often surprised me with how much he knew about my cheer life, and his comment about Leanne was no exception.

"It's going really good actually," I replied. "She's still kind of moody sometimes. But, I've been helping her work on her full, and I think that's helped a lot. Maybe by competition season we could even be friends."

"You? Friends with a super Barbie cheerleader? I'll believe it when I see it."

"Me too," I agreed with a laugh. "I really think it could happen though. When she got moved from point stunt she didn't even mind. I mean, I thought she was going to glare at me all the time or make rude comments like last season. But then instead, she just told me she was okay with everything if it meant we had a strong team for competition season."

"Sounds like she's super focused on Worlds already," he noted.

"Exactly," I nodded. "After being one of the causes for Nitro's deductions during the finals last year I think Leanne has really matured. Or at least that might be part of the reason. It could also be thanks to all the killer pool parties we're going to have all summer."

"Do I get to come to at least one of them?" Peter made a show of giving me his best puppy dog face.

"Of course," I said immediately. "Everyone's so used to seeing you at competitions I'm sure you'll fit right in."

A strong gust of wind blew across our campground, causing me to immediately shiver. Across the fire from us, Kyle frowned for a second then went back to playing a game on his tablet. Clearly even cold weather couldn't keep him from destroying aliens, or building cities, or whatever his game of the week entailed. Reaching my hands out and leaning forward in my seat in hopes of getting a little more warmth from the fire, I was disappointed as another even bigger gust of wind rolled through.

"Why don't you get a sweater?" Peter asked, clearly having seen my reaction to the colder air.

"I forgot to pack one," I admitted, trying to keep my voice down.

"How did you forget a sweater?" Peter ask, his voice much louder than I wished it would have been in that moment.

"That's what happens when you pack after cheer practice instead of beforehand like someone suggested," my dad replied from across our camp site. He was sitting at a picnic table playing a game of cards with Peter's parents, and had clearly overheard. Thankfully, even through the dim light of the campfire, I could see he was smiling as he made the comment.

"You can borrow mine," Peter offered, then stood up and went to his tent. He returned with a grey hoodie with 'Cardinal Football' written across the chest in red and white letters, complete with an image of the red mascot. "Here you go."

"Thanks, you're a lifesaver."

"Someone's got to look out for you Max," he smiled, then brought up something I wasn't expecting. "So, what's going on with your Instagram fame all of a sudden?"

"Nothing," I said, hoping he wouldn't press the issue.

"You have a thousand followers more than me now," Peter tried again. "That's not nothing and you know it."

"It's all kind of weird," I said with a sigh. "Connor posted a video of me doing some tumbling and suddenly it was shared by a few cheerleading accounts and people freaked out. It's all been really nice and supportive so that's been cool. But, I just wasn't expecting all the follows and comments to start flooding in so suddenly. Especially after my kick double. Once it was posted I got a bunch of comments and a ton of direct messages. People were asking me for shoutouts and then this one lady who sells bows was asking me if I wanted to be a brand embassy."

"Brand embassy?"

"It's called something like that," I shrugged.

"You mean an ambassador?" he asked, laughing when I finally nodded in agreement. "That means they want to send you free stuff since a lot of people see your posts. You should do it."

"But I don't get it," I finally explained. "I'm not anyone special. Like, there are a lot of other people out there who can tumble and cheer better than me. Why does anyone care about me?"

"Maybe they see that you're different from everyone else." Peter clearly saw my confused face and decided to continue. "You're not like most cheerleaders. I mean, just look at this trip. You're out fishing and cooking over a fire. I bet not many other cheerleaders out there do this in their free time."

"I guess so," I began slowly. "I'm still just getting used to all the attention."

"Well, you better get used to it fast," he suggested. "If people are this excited when you're just starting the season on Nitro, they're going to freak out even more when the season starts and you win NCA and Worlds."

I was once again reminded how much about cheer Peter really knew. Bringing up the two largest competitions of the season was not something I was expecting from him. Although at that point it should have been no shock at all. He was my best friend and was always there for me, even about little things. It made me happy to know that he was finally going to be home for the rest of the summer, and that I was getting to spend some fun time camping with him before we headed back into the real world.

"Just remember me when you're rich and famous," Peter added, making me doubt instantly just how 'real' the world back home was becoming.

CHAPTER 22

Friday morning we reluctantly packed up the rest of the camp site and headed home. It was a long drive, and I slept most of the way, still comfy and warm in Peter's hoodie. I offered to give it back to him, but since it was just starting to rain as we left he assured me he would get it later. So, I climbed into the car, plugged in my phone to charge since it was dead, then fell right to sleep. Cars always helped me doze off, and knowing I would need energy for Nitro practice once I got back to town, I was glad for some extra rest.

"Hey Max?" my dad's voice said, waking me after what felt like only a few minutes in the car. When I mumbled nonsense in reply to let him know I was awake he continued. "You might want to wake up, we're almost home."

Sitting up, I stretched and let out a big yawn before looking out the car window. Through the light rain that was still falling I could tell we only had a few blocks left to drive. I knew that trying to get another few minutes of sleep was pointless, so I picked up my phone and was shocked at what I saw. I had dozens of missed texts and calls from Lexi and Halley, as well as a few from Matthew, Connor and Emma. I tried to scroll through them, but nothing they were saying made sense.

A few of the messages mentioned Instagram, so I pulled up the app and had more notifications waiting for me than ever before. I had friend requests, comments, photo likes, and a few dozen private messages. All of it was a lot to process, so as our car pulled into our driveway I decided it could wait. Whatever was causing the excitement would still be there after I unloaded the car, showered, and got ready for cheer. Besides, I had uploaded a video of my attempts at the Arabian before leaving for camping so the new notifications were probably about that.

"Want a ride to the gym?" my dad asked once I had put on my running shoes and was loading an extra protein par into my cheer bag.

"Sure," I grinned, happy for an excuse to avoid pedaling across town.

"Do you plan on wearing that hoodie during practice?" he asked as we climbed into the car.

"No," I assured him. "I just want to stay dry and warm until all the running begins."

"Maybe you'll skip the run because of the weather," he offered, which I quickly shut down.

"Future World Champions don't get worried about a little rain," I said simply.

"Good point," he agreed with a laugh.

My phone continued to go off as we made our way to the gym, but the texts, group messages, and notifications were overwhelming. Knowing I was going to see most of the people trying to contact me shortly, I put my phone on silent and slipped it into my gym bag. It would be there when I was done with practice, and for the time being that would have to be good enough. Or so I thought.

"Did you see my messages?" Connor asked, walking out to greet me the second I climbed out of the car. "I've been trying to get ahold of you all morning."

"I was camping," I reminded him, giving my dad a quick wave and goodbye before closing the door. "My phone was dead until I charged it on the way home, but I was taking a nap that whole time anyways. I didn't get much sleep last night. After we made marshmallows Peter and I decided to stay up late and watch for shooting stars. We saw this one that-"

"What about the posts?" Connor quickly said cutting me off.

"Posts?" I asked.

"Yeah, the Instagram stuff?"

"Oh that," I said with a smile. "Peter and I talked about it and he was thinking it would be cool for me to accept some of the bows and stuff people are offering me."

"Bows?" Connor echoed. "What bows?"

"A lady wants me to be a brand ambassador for her bow company now," I explained. "I guess it's because of all of my new followers."

Connor stared at me with a rather confused and frustrated look on his face. I wanted to ask him what was going on, but my dad and I had arrived at the gym a lot later than we were planning. With only enough time to put my stuff away before practice was set to begin, I raced to my cubby and pulled off Peter's hoodie. I was wearing a shirt sleeve Nitro shirt on under it, knowing the rain would cool me off enough that I wouldn't need to wear just a sports bra.

"Something smells like campfire," Addison commented from her spot standing near the cubbies as well.

"That's my hoodie," I told her instantly. "Well, Peter's really. But the smell is from camping."

"Max," Connor said, reaching out to grab my wrist to get my attention again. "You really need to see this."

Before I could take a look at what he had pulled up on his phone, TJ called out that it was time to begin our usual three mile run. Connor slowly let go of my wrist with a long sigh, then turned to put his phone away. I knew something big must have been going on, but right as we were beginning practice was clearly not a good time to chat. There would be plenty of time to look at what he needed to show me later, so I turned and followed the sea of teal clad athletes outside. The rain was still coming down evenly, making it a slower start for everyone. Even fast runners like myself and Matthew were moving slower than usual to get used to the slick cement under foot.

"Hey Max, welcome back," Leanne smiled, falling into step beside me.

"Thanks," I replied, blinking hard to keep water out of my eyes.

"I came to the gym yesterday and landed the full on the mat," she grinned, her excitement bubbling over.

"That is so awesome," I replied, and honestly meant it.

"I only landed it once though," she admitted. "Maybe at the pool party on Sunday we can practice together on the air mat."

"Great idea," I agreed. "I would offer to stay today to help you but between camping and the party I've got a lot to do."

"No worries," Leanne replied. "How was camping by the way?"

I was a little surprised that she was asking, but at the same time was excited for what felt like a real bonding moment. Leanne wasn't interested in camping, but was willing to listen to my stories about finding animal scat and collecting fire wood. Much like I had told Peter while out in the woods, my once chilly relationship with Leanne was warming up little by little.

"You can go ahead," Leanne said after we were rounding the corner down the street from the gym. "You're never going to beat Matthew if you stay with me the whole time."

"Thanks," I grinned. "I'll see you back in the gym."

Leanne clearly must have seen me keeping a tight eye on Matthew while beginning to speed my pace up ever so slightly. It made me feel a little bad, but it wasn't as intense as my need to finish before my friend and stunt partner. Picking up my pace immediately, I put all of my focus on catching up to Matthew so I could leave him in my dust. So much so, whatever it was Connor needed to show me wasn't even a thought in the back of my mind.

CHAPTER 23

I pushed myself for the rest of the run, enjoying the way the rain cooled me down as my body heated up. Around me I saw other athletes frustrated about the rain, or at least I did until I passed them all. Matthew made a comment about taking it easy as we began the final lap around the block, but I ignored him and pushed on. I knew finishing meant getting out of the rain. Not to mention I wanted to make sure to once again complete the miles before Matthew. Slowing down to push open the door and enter the gym, I glanced back and could just see him turning the corner down the street. The rain had helped me run faster, while slowing him down at the same time. Allowing the door to close behind me, I reached a hand up and felt my now soaking wet hair and bow. With a scowl, I walked to the closest mirror to get a better look at the state of my hair.

"Hey Max," TJ called out, pulling my attention away from my hair. "Go ahead and start conditioning, then warm up tumbling. We have a lot to go over so we're going to rush through everything as much as we can."

"Got it," I said with a sigh, stepping away from the mirror. My bow wasn't sitting how I wanted it to thanks to my floppy wet hair.

"Is everything okay Max?" he asked, raising an eyebrow over my exaggerated sigh.

"Just mad at my hair," I said, pointing to my bow. It was sitting crooked on my head, all while dripping water down the side of my face. "Not to mention, I feel like I swam the three miles today instead of running them."

"Well, you must be part mermaid then," TJ joked. "Your running time is just getting better and better, even with some rain thrown in to trip you up. Matthew is going to need to work a lot harder to catch you."

As if on cue Matthew entered the gym panting harder than usual. He was immediately followed by a few more athletes, and it became clear they had raced the last stretch of the run. I flashed them a smile, glad I still came in first, then went to the mat to begin conditioning. Despite dripping water onto the blue floor under me, I wasn't tired from the run. So, while everyone else took a few minutes to rest or get water before joining me, I was able to get quite a bit ahead. By the time Jade entered the gym around the middle of the pack, I was doing pushups in the corner. She made a beeline for me, looking tired but extremely determined at the same time.

"Did Connor talk to you?" Jade asked as soon as she was closer to me.

"A little," I said, confused by her hushed and serious tone. "I got here a little late thanks to camping."

"Do you know?"

I looked at her standing in front of me in her damp practice wear. Although the rain slowed down as I was finishing my three miles, Jade was pretty soaked. I was glad to see her bow looked like it was in the same wet condition as mine, but that wasn't too important. As I paused in my pushups to sit on my knees, I looked up at her trying to figure out what she could be talking about. Clearly something more than just a few new Instagram followers had happened while I was enjoying some time in nature.

"I don't think so," I finally told her, which made her let out a long sigh. I couldn't tell if the sigh was made in relief or not. But, with a quick nod, Jade turned and moved to the other side of the mat to begin conditioning.

As she walked away, I saw Connor catch her eye and give a little shake of his head. It was strange, but I knew worrying about it wasn't going to do any good. So, I put all my effort into finishing my conditioning and then working on warming up my tumbling as TJ had told me to. I was eventually joined by some other athletes, all of us throwing passes that were a medium difficulty. It allowed our bodies to get ready for harder stunts, and thankfully seemed to give me a chance to dry out a little more.

"Ready for some pyramid work?" TJ asked me as I finally took a break in my tumbling to grab my water bottle.

"Of course," I nodded, causing him to laugh. "What?"

"Is there anything in this gym you're not ready and excited for?" he asked simply.

"Running," I said instantly. "Three miles is enough running in the rain for today."

"Okay, no more running," he assured me. "Just pyramid work."

Once I hydrated, I walked over to the mirror to look at my bow again. It was pretty much dry, but still looked a bit of a mess thanks to my hair. Removing the bow, I ran my fingers through my hair a few times before attempting to style it once again. But, as I was pulling my hair into a super high half ponytail, I was interrupted by Leanne as she came up behind me to help.

"Let me," she offered, taking the bow from my hands.

Moving to stand in front of me she quickly twisted my hair into a bum before expertly putting the bow in its place. I had never made my half ponytail a bun how Leanne had, but instantly loved how it looked. My black and teal bow was sitting perfectly, no longer affected by the small amount of water still in the fabric.

"You need to teach me that some time," I told her, having a hard time taking my eyes off my reflection suddenly.

"Sure," she nodded. "You helped me a lot with my full so giving you help with the girly stuff is the least I can do."

Before we could continue our conversation, TJ called everyone together in the center of the mat. We had worked on the pyramid some, but it was clear the afternoon would focus on just that section of the routine. It meant that everyone had to try the same thing over and over again, and that meant I was constantly being thrown in the air. As the shortest and lightest person, I tried skills time and time again, each of them getting harder and harder as time went on. TJ was clearly trying to see just how far the choreography could push the envelope and raise our raw score for competitions. Thankfully, we made sure to have everyone on hand to spot and base new moves so none of the fliers hit the ground. I was especially thankful, as was Juleah. After all, the bruising on her nose and around her eyes had just faded almost completely away.

Running the same section for what felt like the dozenth time, I was happy to end the Nitro practice time with the completion of a really hard sequence. Standing between Emma and Leanne who were also lifted by their team of bases, I held their arms as I was thrown high for a front flip that landed in a split. Although flips weren't allowed in level 5 flying, since I was holding onto both of the other girls for it, the move was allowed. But, as soon as I was caught in the split I was dropped back down to prep level while I prepared for the next part of the choreography.

As soon as I had completed the assisted front flip, Addison was lifted up to prep level with her back to the audience. Reaching forward, we linked hands, both of our arms crossed over one another to allow for the final skill. Once we counted into the move, I was launched above her head as I kicked my leg up then spun for a kick double down. Granted, all of this was done while also flipping over Addison's head. We held onto one another until a group of bases caught me, allowing me move so I had my feet both cradled and ready for more. I let out a quick breath, then was finally tossed straight up for a toe touch, only to be caught so I was held up by both feet nice and high. Once I had my balance, I reached out to either side to grab Emma's outstretched foot with one hand and Leanne's with the other. Two more fliers were also in the air, and based on the reactions from our coach it looked like everyone stayed in the air. In all, the whole series of skills took a matter of seconds to perform, but was exhausting to say the least.

"Amazing job everyone!" TJ called out, cheering along with all of the athletes on the mat as the fliers were brought to the ground. It was less than half of the full pyramid sequence, and would likely be changed between now and the start of the season, but it felt good all the same. "Hands in everyone!"

After a quick "3-2-1-NITRO!" everyone scattered, still fueled with adrenaline thanks to the hard work leading up to the end of practice. After a quick hug with Addison who thankfully kept me in the air on my assisted kick double down, I turned to look for Leanne. While Addison and I were doing our part in the center, Leanne and Emma were both performing a difficult heel stretch once around, meaning their bases were turning them around in a full circle while they were held on just one foot. It was a move Addison landed right away, but Leanne struggled with. I wanted to tell her congrats on landing it on the last run through, but was interrupted when Jade and Connor both approached.

"Emma said she can give you a ride home," Connor told me immediately, as Jade hooked her arms with mine and began leading me towards my cubbie.

"My dad was going to pick me up," I explained, although I knew he wasn't going to leave the house until I sent him a text. I stayed at the gym after practice often enough that he knew to never assume I was going to be leaving on time.

"Trust me, we need to show you some things," Connor said, bringing my mind back to our conversation at the start of practice.

"It can't be that big of a deal," I said with a shrug, assuring them and myself at the same time.

"Trust me, it's a really big deal" Jade added. "And you need to see it right now."

"Outside," Matthew warned, reaching in out of nowhere to grab the phone Connor was trying to hand me. My friends all shared a knowing look, which left me with a rather unsettled feeling.

"You guys are making me nervous," I said honestly, looking back and forth between them.

When no one immediately assured me it was going to be okay, or that things were only kind of bad, I began to worry even more. But, since Matthew said we had to wait until we were outside I quickly unlinked my arms from Jade's so I could grab my cheer bag and head towards the exit of the gym. I said goodbye to a few people on my way out, stopping to also thank Leanne again for helping with my bow. The second I stepped into the parking lot I was planning to demand someone told me what was going on. But, as I opened the door and saw Lexi climbing out of her mom's grey minivan with Halley by her side the real seriousness of the situation officially set in.

CHAPTER 24

Unfortunately, my friends refused to tell me what was going on until we were sitting in the basement at my house. On the ride there Lexi and Halley asked me about camping and the pyramid work we had done in practice, as if to distract me from what was going on. At the time, it was annoying, but once I was sitting with Connor's phone in my hand I wished we could go back to not talking about the big story my friends had for me.

"I don't get it," I managed, as I scanned photo after photo on Instagram. "Why would anyone do this?"

No one spoke, giving me more time to look at what I never thought I would see. When Connor first handed me his phone I expected to see that I had more followers, or even that someone shared a video or photo of mine to a really big cheer account. But instead I was met with post after post that seemed to have been uploaded to attack me on one level or another.

At first, the photos and videos I saw were not the best, but not too bad at the same time. They were photos of me looking less than great, or even videos of me missing stunts at practices. A lot of them were the recent posts Connor or even the gym had posted to Instagram as well as a few from other friends like Juleah or even Emma. But the farther back I looked at posts, the more shocked I was at what I was seeing. Video and photos began popping up showing me working on stunts and skills at open gym times or even in my extra classes with Greg. Trying to understand where they even came from, it struck me then that they were from not only Instagram posts, but also from things posted to Snapchat. Images and videos that were posted to accounts that were private, often that I assumed would be gone for good. If I knew someone was going to repost my cheerleading fails or my terrible hair and makeup attempts, I never would have sent them to friends or put them on my snap story.

"Where did someone even get these?" I asked, hoping my friends were finally ready to answer.

"Someone had to record them from another phone I think," Matthew explained, pointing to one of the images on the screen. "The photo's not as clear, so it might have been a photo taken of a photo so it didn't send you a notification that someone took a screenshot."

"There are also apps that can record things you open on your phone," Emma added. "I had a friend who posts about fashion all the time and uses the app to record runway shows on her computer and phone."

"But this isn't something like fashion," I said simply, pausing in browsing the photos to look around at everyone who was gathered in my basement.

While I rode to my house in Matthew's Jeep with Lexi and Halley, Connor and Jade climbed into Emma's car as well. We were all sitting in my basement, spread out over the couch, arm chairs, and bean bags in front of the large entertainment system on the wall. After telling my dad we were going to be watching a movie, we put on a random action movie at a low volume while we were chatting. My dad had brought us some snacks shortly after we got to my house, but they were quickly devoured by everyone. Nitro practice was no joke, and no amount of stress or frustration over social media posts could keep us from giving in to our hunger.

"Keep going," Connor said to me, drawing my attention back to his phone. "You need to see the rest of them."

With a sigh, I looked at the screen once again and resumed scrolling down the page Connor had pulled up. I was expecting more videos of me messing up, or even of 'embarrassing' photos from Snapchat. In a way that would have been a welcome sight compared with what I actually saw.

"Wait, this was never posted, was it?" I said out loud, stopping as a photo from a recent Nitro team practice filled the screen. Tapping on the image, I could clearly tell that it was a photo of me throwing up just a few days prior. The image wasn't half as bad as the words I read. The caption of the photo simply read: "Out of shape or eating disorder? You decide!"

"I don't have an eating disorder!" I exclaimed, instantly tempted to throw the phone in my sudden anger. "And I'm not out of shape either!"

"We know," Lexi assured me right away.

"I don't think anyone believes this," Connor added.

"Over a thousand people have liked it though," I noted, then began scrolling down the page again. "Why would someone do this?"

No answer was given, everyone around me quiet as I saw photo after photo from the last few weeks at the gym. They all showed me at key times in practices that allowed for less than kind captions. A photo of me wearing a Nitro tank top while the other girls around me we wore their team sports bras made mention of an eating disorder once again. One video of me messing up choreography in practice suggested I was the weak link on the team. The posts and comments seemed to be endless. Everything was bad but nothing prepared me for the post that left me gasping in shock, as I had to actually turn the phone over to sit facing down in my lap. It was the only thing I could think of doing to prevent seeing the video for a second time.

"What?" Matthew asked. He was across the room from where I was sitting, so he didn't know what post I was responding to.

"It was the stunt fall," Jade said simply.

The stunt fall in question was the one that left me sore and gave Juleah a black eye. Other than minor bobbles or errors, I had never really taken a big spill while stunting.

Especially not while someone was filming. This was the one exception. The video showed the whole fall, and it was a bad one. After I had a second I picked up the phone and watched the video over again, my stomach churning at the images I was seeing.

On the screen, I watched over and over as I began pitching to the left while being held high above the mat. I remembered the moment I started falling, but nothing else. So, seeing myself plummet quickly to the ground with Juleah stepping so she was under me with just seconds to spare was enough to make my heart stop every time. For some reason, I always assumed I had hit Juleah in the face with my arm, something I had done to Halley a few times in the past while in the same stunt group on Blast. But it wasn't my arm that hit her nose, it was the back of my head. If she had not stepped in right when she did, it was clear that my head would have made contact with the mat instead, causing more damage than I even wanted to think about. What made it all worse, however, was the caption posted below. It said simply: "When level 3 athletes are on level 5 teams."

"We should take a break," Connor said, reaching over Lexi to take his phone from me. "This is a lot to take in all at once."

"When did you find it?" I asked him, glad to hand over the phone and all the images still on the screen.

"Yesterday," he replied, tucking his phone into his pocket for the time being. "I saw one of the Snapchat ones randomly then started looking around more."

"A lot of them don't show up on my account," Lexi explained. "They probably won't show on your phone either. I think the account behind all of this has us blocked."

"Is it the same account posting all of them?" Despite looking at the posts, I hadn't paid attention to the account or person uploading all of them.

"They were all first posted by the same account, but I've found them a few other places just without the super rude captions under them," Jade explained. "It looks like that main account posted them first and then sent them around a bunch. Some of them have been shared only a few times, but the one of your stunt fall has been popping up all over the place since last night."

"Why would people want to watch me get hurt like that?" My emotions were a mix of anger and shock as I spoke. "How is that something you should share?"

"Cheer fail accounts post stuff like that all the time, but usually the people in the video know about it," Matthew said. "I posted a tumbling mess up once and an account actually asked if it was okay for them to repost it. Since then I've tagged that account in a few other posts so they could repost if they wanted or whatever."

"But I didn't give anyone permission to post those," I reminded him. "Not to mention someone isn't just posting these things about me. They're saying really terrible stuff about me too. I mean, who would do this?"

"Well, it would have to be someone in the gym," Jade began, her words slower than usual.

"You know, don't you?" I asked her, instantly remembering her attempt to talk to me when she returned from her run during practice.

Jade nodded, then took a long breath. Finally, her eyes locked onto mine before she delivered the blow. "Leanne. The posts are all from Leanne."

CHAPTER 25

I stared at Jade, certain I had heard her wrong. There was just no way Leanne could have been posting things about me over the last few weeks. She was finally being nice to me and becoming my friend. But, when I reminded my friends of all this I began to see just how wrong about everything I really was.

"The posts started a little after Worlds," Connor was explaining. "Which was also just after Summit. Leanne was clearly upset that you won and she didn't, and it looks like she made this account in her anger."

"The posts started to get really bad after that practice when TJ moved you to center flyer," Emma added. "It was like it made her more upset so she started to get really mean. The videos and photos of Nitro practice just started popping up this week though. They were what helped us find the account finally."

"Maybe she felt bad and wanted to finally let people know it was her so she could move on?" The question sounded weak even as I spoke the words.

"More like she knew you were out of town and got sloppy," Jade said with a sneer. "She knew you wouldn't have internet for a little while and was probably hoping when you came home and saw all the posts that you would want to quit cheer or something. But she's wrong about that one."

"Right?" Lexi asked quickly. "You're not going to quit cheer now, are you?"

"I don't know what I'm going to do," I said honestly. I wanted to add that quitting the gym wasn't even an option, but even that felt unclear. "If it really was Leanne, then how did she get those videos? No one was filming during those practices."

"TJ was."

At Connor's words, I was suddenly reminded of the ever-present tripod in the gym during Nitro team practices. The camera was always capturing every moment from the start of conditioning to the final team huddle. It allowed TJ to look back over the practice time and see things he might have missed. Things that could help determine who wasn't going to be staying on the team all season, or what stunt didn't look quite right. Most seasons the camera wouldn't come out until closer to Worlds, but this year was different. This year was all about Worlds, which meant the camera was there since day one. It also meant every moment like me throwing up, missing dance steps, and falling out of my stunt, were captured forever.

"How would Leanne have gotten the videos?" I challenged, not ready to believe she could be behind the posts I had just seen.

"We're not sure," Halley said slowly. "When Connor messaged us about it we tried to figure it out, but that was the part that didn't quite make sense."

"Yeah," Lexi continued. "But it's obviously someone who knows about not only the camera but also when there might be stuff on the videos that could be used to make you look bad."

"But that could be a lot of people, not just Leanne," I said, although I doubted the words even as I said them.

"No, it's Leanne," Jade said with the shake of her head. "Her account has a different name, but it's her."

Before I could ask, Jade explained. I sat and listened to her, shocked at what I was hearing. Apparently, the account that Leanne was using had once been her attempt to share cheer secrets and gets lots of attention on Instagram. She wanted to be a cheerlebrity, and thought making a big account that everyone wanted to follow would help. Unfortunately, she didn't get the fame she was looking for and gave up as she was beginning her first year on Fuze three seasons before. Jade was friends with her at the time, so she knew of the account well.

"Leanne kept complaining that people didn't like her photos or whatever. So, one day a bunch of us all agreed to share the photo to help her get attention. The photo got over a hundred likes so she was really happy, but after another week or two she told everyone she was closing the account. I unfollowed it, and honestly haven't thought about it since then."

There was a time gap that we didn't know about, but it was clear the account was renamed, and a new theme was also added. Posts were made about cheer in general, about drama in cheer gyms, as well as some posts asking people to send in drama from their gyms that she could post. It made sense considering that the account was now named 'CheerDramaLlama.' The name was odd, but it allowed Leanne to post about other gyms around the country, talking about parent drama and even about athletes that were kicked off squads or taken out of certain parts of routines. It was petty stuff, but she gained a lot of followers over time thanks to the content.

"But what does all of this have to do with knowing this is Leanne's account?" I finally asked, not sure I understood what Jade was trying to say.

"The photo we all shared that one day is still on the account," Jade said simply. "For whatever reason, she didn't delete it and it's still there. I don't follow the account anymore since I thought Leanne was closing the account, but it shows I liked the post still. And not just me. Kennedy and Amber-Lynn liked that post too."

I didn't know them personally, but was aware that both girls were on Bomb Squad. I also knew they were two of Leanne's best friends at the gym. Knowing what I was about to ask, Connor handed me his phone once again. I immediately headed to the

CheerDramaLlama account that was posting the worst of the video and photos of me. As Jade had explained the account talked about other gym drama, and featured other athletes failing at stunts and tumbling. It looked like a lot of people were sending in content to be shared. But, when it came to the TNT Force gym, I was the only athlete that was being posted about. Posts that made up easily half of the account's overall content.

Clicking on the first image of myself, I saw it was a collage made of two photos of me, one with Blast and one with Fuze. Both were taken at Summit, our first-place banners making an appearance in both images. Glancing at the time stamp I was planning to do the math on how many weeks ago it was, when I saw the caption. There, under the photo in bold letters that seemed to instantly slap me in the face was written: "Maxine may have two Summit rings, but she doesn't have a mom. So, who's really a winner now?

"Why would she say that?"

My voice came out in a whisper, and in that moment everything seemed to finally hit me. As much as I didn't want to believe that Leanne was behind the posts I was seeing, I knew I needed to believe my friends. They cared about me, and were only giving me the bad news because they knew I needed to see the truth. Leanne, on the other hand, was clearly someone that couldn't be trusted. Not only was she fake to my face, she was saying horribly terrible things behind my back. And not just saying them, putting them out there for everyone to see. She was starting rumors about my health and even my cheerleading ability. Her comment about my mom, however, was the worst thing I could imagine. With my eyes still locked on the photo's caption, I could see the letters blur as my eyes filled with tears that quickly spilled down my face.

"I'm so sorry Max," Lexi said, quickly wrapping her arms around me.

My other friends moved from around the room to also envelope me in a group hug. Their arms around me felt nice in that moment, although it did little to make up for what I had just seen on Connor's phone. But I tried to push those images from my mind and instead remind myself that I had real friends who were there for me in that moment. And, as I heard someone walking down the steps into the basement I knew someone else who cared about me needed to know what was going on as well.

"Max, are you okay?" my dad asked once he reached the bottom of the stairs.

Rather than answer, I untangled myself from my friends so I could stand up and move forward to hug my dad. It was just what I needed in that moment. Even more than my friends, I needed my dad to comfort me and let me know everything was going to be okay. Sure, I didn't know how it was going to be okay, but I was somehow confident that my dad would find a way to get to the bottom of everything I had just learned about Leanne and the posts she had been making online.

CHAPTER 26

Relaying the whole story to my dad was hard, to say the least. I struggled to explain everything, but thankfully my friends took over. They went through the details, showing the posts as we went. I avoided looking at the photos and videos that time around, knowing it wouldn't feel any better seeing them again. If anything, it would make it worse. Thankfully, they were easily avoided and before I knew it we sat waiting to hear what my dad was going to say about everything that had just been laid out before him.

"I'm going to go give the gym a call," he said simply, giving me a quick kiss on my forehead before standing up. He had an extremely serious look on his face and his fists were balled at his sides as he turned to address me and my friends. "Why don't you kids go for a swim or something. Try to have some fun for a little bit. I'll handle all of this."

Everyone seemed to agree with him, including myself. I took in a deep breath in hopes of it helping my overall mood but suddenly felt worse for a different reason altogether. My dad's comment about swimming made me remember the upcoming pool party. In just two days, all of the athletes and parents from Nitro would be over for a fun party. Without knowing the outcome of my dad's call to the gym, I wasn't sure if the get together was going to be such a good idea. Since I couldn't do anything to change things at that moment, I tried to simply move past it and instead distract myself with other things.

"I need to go do some tumbling," I finally announced, hopping up off the couch. "Do you guys want to try out my air mat?"

"Yes!" Matthew and Connor agreed instantly.

"I love that we spend so much time cheerleading, but we still get excited to do even more," Jade commented. "So Max, you think you can teach me to do a kick double?"

"Maybe not today," I said with a laugh. "But I don't see why not!"

As everyone began talking about different tumbling skills they wanted to work on, we headed outside and got the air mat all set up. When it wasn't in use I stored it in my room along the back wall of my closet. I noticed as I grabbed it that my dad was on the phone in his room. For a second I thought about listening in to hear what he was saying, but knew it was better to let him handle things for the time being.

"We should work on partner stunts," Matthew mentioned, once we were outside. Clearly, he was not that interested in tumbling. It made sense since only one person could use the mat at a time, which made for a lot of standing around for everyone else.

"Sure," I replied, knowing it would be a fun change to try new skills. "Everyone needs to help spot though. I don't feel like landing too hard on the grass today."

"I'll spot you guys," Connor quickly volunteered, followed by Jade, Halley, and Juleah. "What skill are you going to try?"

That was the hard part. In partner stunting we hadn't done a lot of difficult things on Nitro yet, since it was a developing skill for some of the partner pairs. Knowing we could try anything we wanted though, Matthew decided to go big or go home.

"Let's do a ball up to heel stretch," Matthew finally suggested. "Then from there we could try an arabesque with a one hand grip."

"One hand?" Jade asked in shock. "Are you sure that's even possible?"

"Max is super light," he shrugged. "As long as she can get her balance under control and I can get the grip right then I think it should be pretty easy."

"And you're up for all of that Max?" Connor asked, although he had a smile on his face since he already knew my answer.

"Of course," I grinned.

Moving to stand in front of Matthew, my back towards him, he placed his hands on my hips then waited until I had a good grip on his wrists. Then, I bent my legs low enough to get a big push off as he lifted me into the air. It didn't go too well from there, since when I went for the heel stretch I started to lose my balance. Knowing I was going to fall, Mathew moved his hands out from under me and reached up to once again grab my waist and help me to the ground.

"Again?" he asked, as soon as I had my feet planted firmly under me.

"Again," I agreed, then got ready to once again be lifted into the air.

We continued like that for a solid hour, trying harder skills that often didn't work. It was fun to really see how far we could push ourselves, and since it was in my backyard it took some of the pressure off. Much like when Leanne had been working on her full. Thinking of working with her earlier in the week was a bad idea, but I quickly pushed it aside in an effort to keep my stress level low.

It was also fun to try out new combinations, although there was no guarantee what the partner stunt sequence of the routine would look like in the end. We had just started working on a string of skills, so everything we did was just to experiment. Not only that, but even if we did land the random things we were trying, there wasn't a good chance a lot of the other pairs on the team could accomplish what we could. As the smallest flier with the strongest base, it was clear we had an overall big advantage.

"Do you want me to film anything to send to TJ?" Emma offered from where she was sitting in the grass.

"I don't think I'm quite ready for any more videos of me going around," I said with a shake of my head. "But if you want to just film and not send or upload them anywhere, that's okay I guess."

Emma completely understood, knowing the situation I was in. So, in the end, she filmed a little but mostly just watched. We tried some really hard skills a few times and also some that were more than likely going to be in the Nitro routine since they were pretty common for competition. It was a good workout either way, and by the time we were done all I could feel were my sore abs from holding my body so stiff and locked while high above Matthew.

"I think I might want to take a break and just do some tumbling," I finally told Matthew.

"Only you would think tumbling is taking a break," Lexi said from her seat on the air mat. "So, can you really do an Arabian and a kick double in the same tumbling pass?"

"Kind of," I shrugged. "I did it once, but I don't know if I can really land it all the time."

"Yet," Connor interjected. "If you simplify your pass to end with a kick single we can work on timing for a bit. Lenny helped me on my Arabian yesterday when I was at the gym."

"Was it for a class?" I asked, trying to remember if there was a higher level tumbling class offered on Thursdays during the summer.

"No," he shrugged. "Just getting some extra practice in while I can. I mean, I can't let you be the only good tumbler on Nitro."

"What about me?" Matthew asked, hopping up from his spot sitting in the grass next to Emma.

"I mean, you're okay at tumbling I guess," Connor shrugged, trying hard to keep a grin off his face.

"Oh, it's on now," Matthew said simply, causing a chorus of "Ooohs," from all of us girls.

For the next few minutes the boys went back and forth competing to see who was the best at tumbling. They tried their hardest passes on both the air mat as well as the grass. Both of them were throwing complicated series of skills, often ending in double fulls or kick singles. The competition was fun, but after a while I knew I needed to end it once and for all.

"Okay, okay," I announced, standing up and moving towards the boys. "Why don't you sit down and let a real cheerleader show you how it's done."

My friends once again let out an "Oooh," before cheering me on. Connor and Matthew both took a seat as I stepped onto the air mat, with the determination to try something I had only worked on once before. I took off, performing a round off and two back handsprings before ending with a full. Then, as

245

soon as my feet hit the ground I performed a punch front, so I could continue the tumbling pass traveling towards where the entire sequence of skills had started from. After the punch front I could tell I was slowing down a little so I did a round off, followed by two back handsprings before I launched my body into the air for a kick double. As soon as my feet hit the ground everyone was celebrating, including both of the boys.

"Since when have you been working on a pass like that?" Matthew asked after giving me a high five.

"I tried earlier this week while I was waiting for Leanne to come over," I said simply. "I'm still not that good at it though."

"You never cease to amaze me," Connor laughed, then pulled me in for a hug.

I returned the hug, then was glad to get back to more tumbling and stunting. Once I worked on tumbling a little more, I decided to rest and sit out for a bit. It was an entertaining break to say the least, since I got to watch as Jade, Matthew, and Connor tossed Emma high in the air to work on some flying. Then, Halley and Emma sat with me as the same group based for Lexi as well. Sitting there watching my friends all work together to try different skills, I was glad they were there for me. I knew eventually I would learn more about what was going on with Leanne from my dad. But, for the time being, the chance to hang out and just have fun with so many of my friends from the gym was exactly what I needed. Although I didn't answer the question when I was asked earlier in the day, I knew even with what I had been shown on Instagram I wasn't going to leave the TNT Force gym. As bad as everything appeared to be with Leanne, my friends more than made up for it. So, if being around them meant I had to also be around people less than kind, it was worth it every time.

CHAPTER 27

"You ready for this?" my dad asked, after finding a parking spot at the gym Saturday afternoon.

"I don't think so," I said with a sigh. "But I know we still need to go in there." My dad leaned over to give me a hug, then we both got out of the car and headed towards the gym entrance.

After quite a bit of time tumbling and stunting in the backyard the night before, my dad ordered dinner for everyone. I had a feeling at least part of it was as a thank you to my friends for being by my side when I needed them the most. Between the long day of practice for everyone on Nitro and the additional work afterwards we were excited for food, and lots of it!

Once we had enjoyed all the taco truck food we could manage to eat, my friends slowly began to head home. Lexi and Halley left with Matthew so they could get stuff and come back over to spend the night. While they were gone my dad explained that he spoke with TJ, Nicole, and Tonya and let them know what was going on. After giving them the information, they made it clear that what was going on was not okay, and they would be taking care of it. The first step in taking care of it involved talking to Leanne and some other athletes in the morning. After that they told my dad they would call us to give an update. The call from the gym came at 2pm, and without giving us much information, they asked us to head the gym. We were in the car within minutes, thankfully not giving me too much time to stress or worry.

"Hey Max," Lenny welcomed me as we walked inside. It was clear he had been standing there to greet us in place of the other coaches. "If you guys can just wait out here for a little bit Tonya will come get you once they're ready."

While Dakota headed across the gym towards where he was working with a few athletes on the tumbling tracks, I glanced at the offices and saw the blinds were all closed.

I could hear people talking inside, but it was impossible to tell what was being said. I also didn't know who exactly was in the office with the three gym owners, but assumed at least one person was Leanne. Although, if everything we thought we found out was wrong, then maybe it wasn't Leanne at all. Maybe someone else was behind everything. I held onto that hope, refusing to accept the idea that all of Leanne's niceness over the past few weeks was fake.

While my dad looked at a cork board with upcoming gym events plastered all over it, I sat down on the mat closest to me and started stretching. It was second nature for me when I was in the gym, so I just allowed my body to do what it was already wanting to do. Sure, I wasn't in cheer clothes, instead wearing grey basketball shorts and a faded red shirt, but it gave me something to do while we waited.

"Max?" I looked up when I heard TJ's voice. "Come on in."

In that moment, I wanted nothing more than to just run and hide in the bathroom like I had done so many months before during the TNT Cheer Camp. But instead, I stood right next to my dad and followed TJ as we walked into the office and took a seat on two chairs that were open for us. Once I sat down I saw that Leanne and her mom were sitting across the room, neither of them looking our way. There were a few other athletes in the room as well, sitting together in chairs near the window. It took me a second to realize they were Kennedy and Amber-Lynn, both of whom had at least some knowledge of the CheerDramaLlama account based on what Jade had shown me.

"Thanks for coming today Max," Nicole said once my dad and I were sitting down. She was behind her desk and had a very serious look on her face. Her curly red hair was pulled into a tight braid that made her already thin and angular face look even more so. "Thank you, Brian, for calling us last night and letting us know about everything that has been going on. As we were just discussing, TNT Force has a zero-tolerance policy for bullying."

"It wasn't bullying!" Leanne's mom all but shouted, and I instantly got the feeling it was not the first time she had said the statement. "Some photos showed up online and Max got her feelings hurt. Big deal. My daughter has had videos and photos of last years' Worlds performance posted everywhere and no one seemed to care at all!"

There was a silence that hung in the room after her statement. Looking around, I saw that Leanne was staring at the ground, her jaw set in what I could only assume was anger. I had a feeling that the silence was going to go on forever. Thankfully my dad finally spoke up and ended the silence once and for all.

"Am I correct to assume that we have found the guilty parties responsible for the posts in question?" he asked, sounding every bit like the doctor he was.

"Yes," Tonya nodded simply. She was sitting on a chair in the corner with a pen and notebook resting on her lap. I had a feeling she was likely making notes of things. It was something I saw people do in courtroom scenes on TV, and had a feeling that recording what was going on was a good idea.

"No one has admitted anything," Leanne's mom reminded everyone in the room. Her tone was still very much on edge.

"I admitted things," Amber-Lynn said in reply. "So did Kennedy."

"Yeah," Kenny nodded. "And Max, we're really sorry. Sometimes not doing anything to stop bullying is just as bad as being a bully yourself."

"Oh," I just barely managed, her statement catching me off guard. "I appreciate you saying that. And I forgive you."

My dad also thanked the girls for their apologies, then Nicole told them that they were free to go. Even though I didn't know for sure, I had a feeling this meant that they pretty much backed up what my friends had discovered. Especially Jade. This meant that Leanne really was responsible for the posts made about me, even if she wasn't saying it out loud. As the thought sunk in, I was just as shocked as when Jade first suggested Leanne was behind everything.

"Leanne, do you have anything you would like to say?" Nicole asked after Kennedy and Amber-Lynn were out of the room. Her eyes were all but drilling holes into Leanne.

"No."

"Nothing at all?" Nicole tried again.

"No."

The awkward silence was back once again, only this time it was combined with a stare down. The coaches were all looking at Leanne and her mom, who were looking back with such determination and annoyance that I was almost wondering if maybe they really had nothing to do with the Instagram posts at all. But, after what Kennedy and Amber-Lynn said before they left, I knew it couldn't be true. Leanne was to blame, and seeing her have this showdown with the coaches just made it more upsetting. Clearly, she wasn't sorry in the least.

"Max, Dr. Turner, why don't I walk you two out," Tonya finally said.

Everyone else still sat frozen in their staring match as we got up and left the office. As we stepped out into the gym it was as if we walked into a different world. Athletes were going on with practices like nothing was happening beyond the office door. Then again, I didn't know how many of the athletes at the gym knew what was really going on. My friends of course knew all about it, but did other people know already too?

"I'm really sorry about everything," Tonya said, grabbing my attention. "We wanted you here for her to apologize, but it's clear she's not ready to do that just yet."

"It was nice to hear the other girls apologize if nothing else," my dad replied, and I nodded in agreement.

For a second it looked like Tonya was going to say something else, but we were cut off as loud yelling erupted from inside the office. Even with the door shut, the windows closed and covered, and the noise of the gym not far away, their words were clear. Leanne and her mom were not happy with whatever TJ and Nicole had just said, and were yelling everything they could think of to express their thoughts on that matter.

CHAPTER 28

When I was little, I remembered the first time I really heard and understood what a bad word was. My mom and dad had put me to bed, but I wasn't tired for whatever reason. So, instead of trying to fall asleep I snuck to the top of the stairs to see what they were watching on TV. From my spot perched above the family room I heard the actor in the movie they were watching use a word that caused both of my parents to literally laugh out loud. Since I had ever heard the word before, I assumed it was something funny and saved the word in my mind to use when I wanted to make people laugh as well.

The next week at school we were all enjoying a snack time and one of the boys in class was telling a story about his brother that was making the other students in the class laugh. Not to be outdone, I decided it was time to use the word I had heard my parents laugh at. So, just as everyone was quieting down, I said the word nice and loud so everyone would hear. Unfortunately, no one laughed.

In fact, the opposite occurred. My mom and dad were called into school that day and had to sit with me as my teacher explained how I had used the 'f' word in class. It was weird to me that I was getting in trouble for using a word that made them laugh in the past. But my parents explained to me that it was a really bad word. When I still didn't get it, they explained that it kind of meant 'really' or 'a lot.' They also explained that only adults should use it, it was not something for a kindergartener like myself. Over and over again they expressed to me that they didn't want me to ever say it again. And I didn't, until two weeks after my mom died.

After my mom died I was struggling with everything, as was to be expected. So, on a particularly hard day I decided to once again use the 'f-word.' I said it to describe my hatred for the cancer that took my mother from me. Although my teacher was both shocked and unhappy I used the word, she hugged me and had tears in her eyes all the same. She still called and spoke to my father, who reminded me not to use that word. Even as he reminded me, it was clear he wasn't as mad as the time before since I had used it to express my emotions towards cancer and the destruction it had caused in my life. It was clear everyone knew I was going through a lot at that time, so all was forgotten when I assured my dad I would never say it again. And I held true to that promise, making sure that even in anger I kept the word from my mouth.

With that in mind, hearing the 'f-word' flying from the office in the TNT Force gym hit me like a shock wave. Not just because I was certain at least one of the voices saying the word was Leanne, but also because it was combined with a lot of other hateful words and accusations. The voices began to overlap and drown each other out, but I heard my name a few times, as well as what seemed to be some not so nice opinions of me. Thankfully, it ended abruptly, and was followed by Leanne and her mother both storming out of the office and then out of the gym altogether. They were in such a hurry, in fact, that they didn't seem to notice me or my dad standing by as they left.

"Well, that went well," TJ said with a shrug as he finally exited the office.

"That was what it looks like when it's going good?" I asked. "I would hate to see how it would look if it's going bad."

The comment seemed to be just what the moment needed, causing TJ to laugh before walking over and giving me a hug. I was a little confused, but knew that in order for Leanne and her friends to be there when we arrived, the coaches likely had had long chats with them all morning. What I didn't know was just what was said during those conversations.

"Max, we really want to let you know how sorry we are that all of this occurred," Nicole said, also walking over to give me a hug once TJ had let me go. "You are an amazing athlete and a joy to have at this gym. Leanne wasn't ready for the competition you suddenly gave her, and it unfortunately showed in a way we didn't see until it was a little too late."

"So, what's going to happen now?" I asked, looking between the three gym owners for an answer.

"Leanne is no longer a part of the TNT Force family," Tonya said simply.

"You mean she's not on Nitro?"

"She's no longer at the gym at all," TJ explained. "Even before you arrived it was clear that Leanne no longer cared about anyone but herself. We've seen little things in the past, and have even spoken to her about some things. But this was different. This was much worse, and we knew it was the last straw."

"Just like that?" I asked, not really sure if what I was hearing was real.

"Leanne and her mom have been here for quite a while going over all of this with us," Nicole explained. "Once your dad called us we tried to get to the bottom of everything and spent last night looking into a lot of different accounts and posts. But it was about more than that. Leanne didn't just post things, she snuck into TJ's office and stole videos off of his computer. When we realized that, we decided to meet with them as early as possible so we could address that issue. Thankfully she didn't cover her tracks online that well and we could see exactly when she logged on to export the files to her e-mail account."

"Did she admit to any of it in the end?" my dad asked, the same thought I was also thinking.

"No," TJ said with a shake of his head. "But Kennedy and Amber-Lynn told us everything we needed to know. They were both more than happy to help us out and give us the information we needed. We even have some screenshots of messages Leanne sent to both girls about you, proving her motive also matched the timeline of posts."

"Your wins at Summit were what appear to have really set her off," Tonya added. "Until then, she was pretty much just hoping for you to fail. But when both Blast and Fuze won after Nitro didn't make top 3 at Worlds, she really seemed to have it in for you."

I nodded, but it was so much to take in. It had been one thing to assume different things, and even see bits of evidence for it. But to stand there in the gym and hear that Leanne had been plotting against me for months was crazy to think about. Not only that, but I even spent time helping her work on her tumbling. While I had been trying my best to be friends with her, she was trying to use social media to get out her frustrations and bring me down a notch. And it worked. It made me feel terrible. But, unfortunately for her, it also got her removed from the gym.

My dad and I stayed for a little longer to talk to the coaches, then we headed home. On the short drive, I sent a group text to everyone who had been at my house the night before and gave them the news. It was a shortened version, which I assumed would be good enough for a little while. Instead, the questions began pouring in and I had to go over a lot of the details again. Typing them out felt weird and pretty terrible at times. Part of me was glad Leanne was no longer going to be able to treat me the way she had, but another part of me felt bad. She was kicked out of TNT Force, and I felt responsible.

My friends were all shocked at first to say the least. Even after giving them the basic story, they kept asking if it was really true that Leanne had been removed from not just Nitro but the whole gym. I explained the fight before Leanne and her mom left in more details, hoping it would help. Since I didn't know what the conversation was like before I got there, it was all I could offer to my friends. Thankfully it did the job to help the news sink in for everyone.

"Better you than her," Matthew finally said in the group chat. Everyone sent comments agreeing. Then, my phone buzzed again as Connor sent a text to just me, rather than posting in the group conversation.

"This isn't your fault," he had typed.

"I didn't say it was." I tapped out my message slowly, not sure what else to say in reply.

"But I know you, Max," Connor answered back. "You're an amazing person and don't like to see other people in trouble even if they deserve it. Like when Scott was kicked off Nitro. I could tell you blamed yourself a little since he was in your stunt group. But this isn't like that. Leanne dug her own grave on this one."

I had to read his message twice before I could reply. He really did know me better than most other people, including many of the athletes on Nitro. "You're the best Connor."

Connor messaged a reply offering to come over early the next morning to help set up. It was then, as I stared at my phone that I remembered the whole team was coming over Sunday afternoon. Every athlete and their family was invited for the cook out and pool party. That meant I was about to be face to face with the whole team that was now down one flier. All thanks to things she had posted about me. The thought had my stomach churning even thinking about it. So, after explaining that Connor was welcome to come over as early as he wanted, I turned off my phone and went outside to work on tumbling using my air mat. I only hoped it would work as well as the day before at getting my mind off everything.

CHAPTER 29

By Sunday morning I was feeling a little more at ease about the Leanne situation. Enough so that I finally logged back onto Instagram. I had missed a lot of posts from friends, as I was expecting. What I was not expecting, however, was that I had even more followers and likes and comments than ever before. It was confusing at first, but then I saw that all my friends at TNT Force had shared a post about me that was started by Connor.

The post was a photo of me being held high above Matthew in my backyard from Friday afternoon. The picture was a little hard to make out since over it was a whole paragraph asking accounts to take down photos that were mean or hurtful to me, explaining that I had been the victim of cyberbullying recently on Instagram. The message also had a request to share the post in an effort to help inform people about what had happened. The posts also included the hashtag #TNTForceMax. When I clicked on the hashtag, I was floored to see dozens of copies of that original post pop up, as well as many more people using the hashtag when they shared other photos and videos of me from my page and my friends' accounts.

All of it was enough to make me tear up as I raced to find my dad and show him. I had to then help him make his own Instagram account so he could be a part of the fun. Worry set in that I would have to spend the whole morning helping him upload hundreds of photos, but when my friends arrived I was instantly off the hook.

"Connor, you're the best!" I announced, jumping onto him the second I saw he was standing on the doorstep. Despite sending him a few text messages, I felt the need to say it in person as well.

"You two are adorable," Emma laughed, walking past both of us and into my house. "Where should I put everything?"

Finally letting go of Connor, I grabbed some of the bags Emma was carrying and took them into the kitchen. Although we had worked on most of the crafts together, she had also been working on some items at home on her own. We quickly unpacked the snack bags, supplies for the decorate-your-own-cheer-bow station, and finally the rest of the balloons and streamers we needed to use around the pool deck. We knew that Matthew would be coming over with Lexi and Halley soon enough, and wanted to make as much progress before they arrived.

"Do you think people are going to be mad when they see Halley is here?" Emma asked as we worked as a team to blow up balloons with the helium tank my dad had bought. "I mean, I know families were invited, but she doesn't really have a sibling on the team."

"If anyone asks she is my sister for the day," I replied with a shrug. "Besides, with Lexi coming with Matthew it wouldn't be fair to leave Halley out."

"Good point," Emma smiled. "And I'm for sure not complaining. The more help on these balloons the better."

"Do you know if anyone isn't coming?" Connor asked, although I knew immediately he was hinting at something specific from the way he asked the question.

"Who are you wondering about?" I challenged him, pausing in adding ribbon to a balloon.

"Tess," he said simply.

I should have guessed he would mention her, since she was Leanne's best friend on Nitro. Although Kennedy and Amber-Lynn were closer with her, since they were both on Bomb Squad Leanne spent most of her time with Tess. In a lot of ways Tess reminded me of a little Leanne wannabe with her hair and makeup styled just like Leanne's every day. The only different was that Tess was a few inches taller and was better suited to be a base than to fly. She was still what most people would call 'thin,' but just not quite thin enough to be tossed in the air. If it wasn't for their different build and Tess's braces, they could pass as twins. As it was, I'd heard a few people ask them if they were sisters at competitions.

"I'm assuming she'll be here," I finally said. "But I don't know. We have enough food for all of the Nitro families and about half of the rest of the gym, so whoever shows up I just hope they're hungry."

Proud at how I had sidestepped the question, I looked over and saw Connor was still watching me. Emma had gone back to work on filling the balloons, but Connor could tell something was wrong. Exactly what was wrong, I didn't really know myself. It was almost as if I had nerves and worries building up in me even thinking about the team showing up. Much like the post my friends had made to Instagram, I knew Leanne must have also gotten the word about what happened to her friends. Whether it was the truth or what she wanted to be true, I didn't know. I just hoped that all of it wouldn't affect the team or the swim party.

"Reinforcements have arrived," my dad announced as he opened the sliding glass door so Matthew, Lexi and Halley could join us on the deck. I was happy for their help and very happy for the iced coffees they began passing out. But, mostly, I was happy for the distraction. Putting aside thoughts about Heather, I began helping my friends put out teal table cloths, all while Connor kept an eye on me from across the yard. Clearly, he was more aware of my mood than I wanted him to be in that moment.

With my resolve to not think too much about everything with Leanne or how it might affect the rest of Nitro, I focused on finishing decorating. We worked hard to cover the deck, yard, and even the kitchen in teal, silver, and blue. All the while my dad was busy getting food out on the serving tables and meat on the grill. The hard work of getting everything in place and ready made the time fly by fast, and before I knew it we were greeted with the arrival of TJ and the other members of Nitro.

"This place looks perfect," TJ said in shock as he walked out of the house and onto the pool deck.

"It's all Emma," I told him honestly. "She was the master party planner, I just provided the pool."

"Well, I love it all," he assured me, giving me a quick side hug. "This is going to be great."

I couldn't agree with him more as athletes began enjoying the pool as well as the tables full of food and snacks my dad had baked and bought. My friends quickly made their way into the water, and got right to launching me into the air. Considering the other times they were over for swimming, it was the natural activity to try. Not to mention it was entertaining to the parents that were taking photos in between hanging out with one another. The party was just as much a chance for the adults to spend time together as it was for the athletes, most of whom were either in the pool or sitting along the edge with their feet in the water.

"You want to try that kick triple again?" Matthew asked me, referring to the basket toss we had tried not long ago. It had left me with a faceful of water on the first attempt.

"Let's try it," I nodded, swimming to stand between him, Connor, Nick, and Aaron.

Once Emma was out of the deep end where they had just launched her, we counted down and I flew high into the air. After completing a backflip motion, I kicked my leg up nice and high before whipping my body around in three spirals before entering the water feet first. It wasn't as gentle of a landing as I wanted since there was a small splash spreading around me. But, it was much better than the initial attempt not long ago. Even from under water I could hear people celebrating, only truly realizing how many people were cheering us on once I made it to the surface.

"Looks like Max is the best flier now that she got rid of Leanne."

The sudden comment made me pause as I swam back to the shallow end. I quickly glanced to see who it was that had spoken, but it was impossible to be sure who it was. There were so many athletes and parents in the direction that the comment had come from, leaving me feeling instantly more paranoid. Either way, what I did know was that my fears and worries were coming true. Word had gotten around that I was at least part of the cause for Leanne leaving the gym, and people weren't happy about it.

"Ready to go again?" Connor asked once I was close to where him and the other bases were waiting.

"I think I want to take a break," I said, then quickly exited the pool before anyone could press me for more details.

Walking quickly, I was in my room and closing the door before I even knew where I was heading. I took a few deep breaths and tried to calm down, but I couldn't seem to shake the feeling that everyone at the party was faking it. That they were all pretending to have fun, while quietly judging me. I worried they were all just waiting for me to quit the team so Leanne could come back to the gym. Part of me knew it was crazy to think that way, but I just couldn't push the thought aside.

CHAPTER 30

"Max?"

Hearing Lexi's voice in the hallway outside my bedroom I let out a sigh, then immediately moved to open the door. I was a little startled when I saw her standing there with both Halley and Tonya, but let them all in just the same. All three of them had been there for me through some pretty rough times at the gym, so knowing they were already there for me with the new situation I found myself in was a relief to say the least.

"Is everything okay?" Tonya asked. I took a seat on my bed, Lexi and Halley sitting next to me immediately. "We're a little worried about you Max."

"It's maybe-," I paused, not sure how to say what I was feeling.

"Just tell me the truth," she reminded me, reaching out to rest her hand on my shoulder.

"What if everyone on the team hates me for Leanne leaving? What if they all blame me and want me gone and agree with everything she had to say? I mean, none of them know what happened, so what if they think I did something to get her kicked out of the gym?"

Once I was done talking Tonya frowned, then leaned in to hug me. For a second I was mad she didn't tell me I was wrong, that it wasn't all my fault. But then, I realized that the hug was her way of saying exactly that. Then, she finally let me go and stood up, wiping a tear from her eye as she did.

"Max, I'm sorry for all of this," she said sincerely. "What you had to go through with Leanne wasn't fair. She said some terrible things about you and about your family. Things that made it easy for us to make the decision to remove her from the gym when she didn't apologize for her actions. But now I'm still sorry. Sorry that anyone could doubt why Leanne left, or in any way make you feel like you did anything wrong. You did nothing wrong, and I don't want anyone to make you feel like it was someone other than Leanne who was responsible for her leaving."

"But people don't know," Halley said simply. "Max told some of us about what happened, but I don't think anyone else knows the story. Or at least not the real story."

"Maybe we need to change that."

Before I could even ask what she had in mind, Tonya gave me another fast hug then turned and left my room, closing the door as she went. I was instantly nervous she was going to go just announce things to anyone willing to listen, but then thought better of it. Tonya was like a big sister to me, and in some ways a motherly figure at the same time. She took me to get my haircut when I was in need, and always checked to see if I needed help on girly things like my makeup and cheer uniform. But on top of that, she truly cared about me. Ever since the first time I cried in her office explaining that I was afraid I would never fit in at the gym, she was one of my favorite people at TNT Force. So, trying not to worry until I saw just what Tonya was up to, I turned to my best friends.

"Sorry," I said, not sure how to express exactly how I felt for racing out of my own party.

"You have nothing to be sorry about," Lexi assured me instantly.

"I just feel bad you guys had to leave the party and come find me and all that," I tried again, although I was thankful to have them with me all the same.

"Connor was actually the one who told us something might be wrong," Halley explained.

"Yeah," Lexi added. "I thought you were just hungry or something. But then he said you looked upset when you left the pool. He just didn't know why."

"I overheard some people talking about me," I quickly filled them in. "After my last trick they were saying that I was the best flyer since I got Leanne kicked off the team."

"What?" Lexi asked.

"Who said that?" Halley also asked.

"I don't know. But clearly Leanne has been telling people her side of the story."

"Should we go back out there?" Halley finally asked, after we all sat there in silence for a few moments.

Nodding in agreement, we all stood up and made our way back outside. Not wanting to jump back into the pool right away I walked over and grabbed a cupcake from the dessert table. Lexi and Halley stuck by my side, also taking the time to enjoy something sweet to snack on. Turning away from the table I wasn't too surprised to see Connor walking towards me.

"Hey," he said simply, grabbing a cupcake then moving to stand next to me. "What's up?"

"Just having a snack," I said with a smile. Then, bumping my shoulder into him I added, "Thanks Connor."

"Of course," he smiled down at me. "I'll always be right here for you Max. Not matter what."

Our conversation was instantly cut short when TJ clapped the familiar rhythm that was often heard around the gym. Everyone repeated the claps, quieting down and turning to face TJ. He was standing in the grass with Tonya, who gave a reassuring smile when she made eye contact with me.

"I just wanted to take a little bit of your time real fast, to first of all, say a big thank you to the Turner's. This party has been a great afternoon, and we are all very thankful for you having everyone over." TJ paused while everyone clapped and cheered in agreement. Once everyone quieted down he continued. "If I could please have all the athletes gather around, we need to have a little bit of a team meeting. Athletes you can take a seat here, and families feel free to join us as you would like as well. After all, you are all a very important part of your child's time at the gym."

As athletes began climbing out of the pool or setting their food plates aside and moving towards TJ, I found myself frozen on the spot. This was it. This was the moment where TJ was going to let everyone know about everything that had happened. It was sure to help people know the truth, but it didn't mean everyone was going to be okay with that truth. Since, after all, Leanne was gone and nothing was going to change that. Even if it was caused by her actions, there were sure to be people that were still not pleased with the end result. All of it scared me more than I wanted to admit.

"Are you ready for this?" Connor asked me, wrapping an arm around my shoulders.

"I'm not sure," I said honestly. "But it's now or ever I guess."

Giving Lexi and Halley my best attempt at a brave smile, I walked with Connor across the deck and into the grass. I grabbed a towel on the way, suddenly feeling rather exposed in my royal blue bikini. Wrapping the plush fabric around my body was like a layer of instant comfort, on top of Connor who was still all but glued to my side.

"Over here," Emma called out to me when I finally reached the spot where the other Nitro athletes were sitting down. Connor and I instantly moved to sit with her, noticing Jade, Matthew, Juleah, and Nick were also sitting by them as well.

"Alright everyone," TJ began once a few more athletes had also taken a seat in the grass. "We have some things we need to discuss. A lot has happened since practice Friday afternoon and I want everyone to have a chance to understand why those things occurred. I'm sure a lot of you have heard rumors or comments or maybe even think you know the truth. Well, I want to give everyone a chance to hear the story, to ask questions if needed, and hopefully understand why certain choices were made. After this if you still have questions or concerns you can talk to me in private, but right now I just want us to get everything out in the open in hopes it can help us to continue to become, and to remain, a united team."

I held my breath for what I knew was coming next. Sensing my nervousness Connor reached out and placed a hand on top of mine in the grass. Turning my wrist over, I gripped his hand. He squeezed my fingers in reply as TJ began the story I knew far too well.

CHAPTER 31

"As I'm sure many of you know, Leanne is no longer a member of Nitro, nor is she a part of TNT Force," TJ began simply. "Due to her actions in the past as well as her actions most recently she was asked to permanently leave the gym. If you have any questions about this decision I would be happy to answer them and help us all hopefully get closure on this whole situation."

"Who's going to fill her spot?" someone called out.

"We're not sure yet," TJ said honestly. "We will be working on that in the next few weeks. Someone might swing over from Bomb Squad, or we might pull up someone from Fuze. Or we may begin training another flier to fill her role in the routine. It might take a little while to figure it all out, but we are confident we will be able to get through this as a team."

"Will she ever come back?" another athlete asked.

"No," came the reply. "She is no longer welcome to cheer at the gym again or attend any gym functions until further notice. This is not something the staff sees changing anytime soon based on the manner in which she left."

Much like in the office the previous morning, my backyard suddenly went quiet. I had the feeling there were a lot of people that had questions they wanted to ask. But considering that they were sitting with me, at my house no less, it was awkward to say the least. Finally, someone spoke up.

"Why was she kicked out of the gym?"

I turned and saw it was a parent that asked the question. I didn't know whose mother it was, but based on her tone and the expression on her face I got the feeling she was likely friends with Leanne's mother. This fact was confirmed when she glanced my way after the question and raised one eyebrow before looking back at TJ.

"There were a few reasons," TJ began. "In the past Leanne has displayed a very poor attitude when her squad loses and she has talked back to coaches on more than a few occasions. She also had made comments or remarks to other athletes that bordered on bullying in the past. We have documented all of this over the last few years, just as we document everything that occurs in the gym that requires a coach to talk to an athlete or issue warnings due to their actions of behavior."

"So you just decided out of nowhere to remove her for things in the past?" The mother was clearly challenging TJ. Thankfully, he was not fazed by her in the least.

"On Friday evening, the other gym owners and I became aware of additional infractions Leanne made in the past few weeks," he said in reply to the additional question. "Leanne made an account on social media and was using it to post negative and hurtful things about an athlete at the gym. She chose to attack the other athlete in a way that crossed the line and goes against everything we try to instill in our athletes, especially those on senior teams. The account was made in secret, but recently posts have also been shared around to other accounts as well. The photos and videos were used to attack an athlete at a personal level, or to put it more simply, were cases of truly unwarranted cyber bullying."

"So people can't post about someone they don't like without getting kicked out of the gym?" This questions from Tess, which was no surprise to me.

"No," TJ assured her. "Many of the photos and videos Leanne uploaded to social media were taken from my personal computer without permission. At some point within the last week she broke into the office and went onto my computer in order to send the files to her personal e-mail account. That account was linked to the Instagram page where the posts were found. We were able to uncover proof of this on my computer, which alone is grounds for expulsion from the gym, even without the things she chose to post about the athlete in question."

"You mean Max?"

There was a long pause following the question, which had also been asked by Tess. I squeezed Connor's hand as tightly as I could until TJ answered. "Yes. The athlete Leanne posted about was Max."

"I have a question," a voice near the back said. I turned to look and saw it was my dad. "What is being done to ensure that this level of cyber bullying does not happen to anyone else in the gym? Will there be consequences in the future if anyone is making comments about athletes regarding their physical appearance, health, or family?"

"Absolutely," TJ replied, a smile playing on his lips. Without saying it directly, my dad had just hinted about the posts Leanne made. The response was immediate as parents shifted uncomfortably to look at TJ to hear the answer. "The staff at TNT Force are planning to keep a close eye on the social media pages of all athletes on all teams. We are also working to draw up a contract that all athletes will be required to sign. It will include the gym's anti-bullying policy and explain that if someone knows of an athlete being bullied and does not report it they will be disciplined along with the bully." TJ paused to let it sink in. "What happened to Max is not the first time we have seen bullying in the gym. But this was the first time someone chose to cross the line in this way. Because of that we are making sure it does not happen again. We value each and every athlete that walks into our doors, and have a lot of people who consider TNT Force a second home. I for one feel like the gym is more of a family than an athletic center. So, when a part of that family chooses to do anything to make another part of that family feel hurt to the level Leanne chose to do so to Max, I have no tolerance for it."

After a pause, a voice finally asked, "Have the posts been taken down?" While others turned to see who had asked it, I simply watched TJ through the tears filling my eyes.

"Yes," he answered, giving me a slight nod. "They were all reported and the account Leanne was using was shut down. We have also made an effort to get the accounts who shared the negative photos and videos to also take their posts down and have gotten a good response so far. Most people we have talked to have been more than helpful once we explained the gravity of the situation to them."

After that, only a few people had questions, mostly about what they could do to help. It appeared that my dad allowed people to understand the kind of posts Leanne had made as well as how it felt as a parent to go through what he had been through. Even the mom with the permanent sneer on her face seemed to soften after my dad's questions. But as great as all of that was, hearing just how much TJ was doing to make sure I was the last person at the gym that was bullied was amazing.

"Well, if there are no more questions I think we can get back to the party," TJ finally said, and I saw many people nodding their heads in agreement. "This season is going to be a long one, with a lot of bumps along the way. Big bumps and little bumps and everything in between. My hope is that this bump is behind us and we can move on and become a better team because of having gone through it. Now let's get all hands in for a Nitro on three."

Standing up I was wrapped in a hug by Connor instantly. Working hard to blink away the tears still filling my eyes, I hugged him back as I felt more arms wrap around me. At first it was just Emma, Jade, and Juleah joining the hug. But then, it was followed by Matthew, Nick, Addison, and others nearby. In fact, before I knew it the whole team was enveloping me in a massive group hug. After the hug stretched on for a few seconds, everyone began reaching their arms out towards me, making me the center of the team huddle. Although seemingly a small gesture, in that moment it was exactly what I needed.

"Alright everyone, let's do this," TJ finally called out from his spot near the outskirts of the hug. We all joined in then, our voices extra loud as we did the simple team cheer.

"3-2-1-NITRO!"

ABOUT THE AUTHOR

Dana Burkey is a self-published author living in
 Washington State. Although she is from Ohio, she has been enjoying life in the Pacific Northwest for the last 7 years. Before moving to Washington, Burkey attended college in Ohio where she majored in theater with a minor in creative writing. Burkey works full time in camping, spending her days with K-5th graders. She began self-publishing her YA romance novels in August of 2014, hoping to write stories that can be enjoyed by YA readers of any age. Her books feature a lack of swearing, drinking, and sex, in an effort to allow younger readers to connect with her stories without bad influences. Burkey is currently working on a few projects, which she is looking forward to sharing with readers soon!

Own the cover bow! Check out Sweet Angel Dream Bows on Etsy and order your custom bow today!

SNEAK PEEK

Continue reading for a sneak peek at Dana Burkey's Middle grade Romance, The Kiss Dare! For more information about this book and others, or to rate the book you just read, be sure to check out Dana on Goodreads or Amazon.

Chapter 1

"See you at lunch," I called to Penny, only half paying attention to my hands as I fumbled with my locker combination. I had long since memorized the twists and turns to open it, pulling at just the right moment and causing the metal door to swing open.

With a flurry of activity, I watched as a small black envelope fell from the top slots of my locker. It floated to my feet where I stared at it, wishing it would vanish. Knowing it was only a matter of time before someone else noticed it as well, I slammed my foot over it, blocking it from any prying eyes. I glanced around me to make sure no one was watching as I loaded my book into my messenger bag. Then, leaning down to pretend to tie my shoes, I slipped the envelope out from where it was concealed and tucked it into the bottom of my locker. Slamming the door as I stood up, I raced to first period despite there still being several minutes until the first bell would ring.

It was not until well after I slid into my desk that I felt my breathing return to normal. My heart was still racing faster than usual, but I no longer felt like I might throw up. Slipping the hair tie off of my wrist, I pulled my hair into a low ponytail. The short blond locks barely stayed in place, but having them out of my face helped me to cool off a little more. I wiped the sheen of sweat from my forehead, then pulled out my notebook as Mr. Forrester began talking to the class.

I took notes absentmindedly, my thoughts fixated on the small black envelope in my locker. No one I was friends with had ever gotten one, so why was I suddenly being pulled into this game? Maybe game is the wrong word for it. When you're a beautiful cheerleader and get a note daring you to kiss a football player or even kiss a freshman, it's a game. When you're a popular guy on student council and you're dared to kiss someone that rides the same bus as you, or kiss a girl that's in your third-period class, it's a game. But when someone like me gets a black envelope, it's no longer a game.

Knowing I couldn't change anything at that point, I became determined to not let it get to me. Instead, I focused as hard as I could on history class. I followed along in the book and wrote down each and every word Mr. Forrester wrote on the board. Next, in math, I did extra problems on my worksheets to keep my mind from wondering.

Making up extremely difficult equations to go along with the work we were already doing gave me something to focus on. Then, in choir I tried to hear each and every note of the piano as I sang along with Mrs. Kellerman. I usually just floated by in that class, but anyone sitting near me that day would have thought singing was my favorite thing in the world. I tried and retried to hit every single note each time we went through the song.

When the bell rang at the end of class, I instantly felt my heart speed up. Either before lunch or after lunch, I would need to go to my locker for my afternoon books. Should I take the time and look at what was in the envelope? Would knowing the dare make it any easier? Putting it off a little longer, I went to the restroom before heading to the lunch line. I didn't want to get to my lunch table before Penny or Trent. If I could just enter into their conversation, then it would keep me from having to put in too much effort.

"-he is going to be so mad if she actually kisses him!" I heard Penny say when I was a few feet from the table.

"She has to," Trent shrugged, popping some grapes into his mouth. "That's how the dare works."

Immediately I wanted to run and hide. It was clear they were also talking about the stupid dare. Okay, any other year I wouldn't have said it was stupid, but now that I was a part of it, I didn't like anything about it!

"Who are you talking about?" I asked. I in no way actually wanted to know, but if they kept talking, it could give me some time to think through what I should say.

"Courtney got her dare this morning, and it says she has to kiss an ex," Trent explained while brushing his shaggy brown hair out of his eyes. That was all he really needed to say, thankfully. The rest was filled in with my knowledge of school drama.

Courtney Morris was in our grade and was currently dating Jackson Hill. They started dating right at the start of middle school and were determined that they would keep dating all the way through college into marriage. Everyone knew it was a real possibility-they were basically a celebrity couple at Central Grove Middle School. In fact, they were so close that most people forget that Courtney actually dated Jackson's best friend Scott the first few weeks of 6th grade. It was something that was more or less just forgotten, but now that the kiss dare was out in the open, Courtney would have to basically cheat on her boyfriend if she didn't want to pay the consequences.

"Can someone really make her do that?" I asked, shocked that someone would have the guts to give her that dare after her and Jackson had been together for almost two years now.

"I guess so," Penny replied. "In fact, I bet Scott was the one who gave her the dare in the first place!"

"No way!" Trent shook his head. "I think it was totally Heather. She's had a crush on Jackson forever."

While my two best friends began debating who could have been responsible for daring Courtney to kiss her ex, all I could think about was the dare that was waiting for me. Once I opened the card in my locker, I would only have until the end of the dance on Friday to complete whatever the card told me to do. The part of it that I didn't understand was who would have placed it in my locker to begin with. Sure, it was a tradition at our school for years, but generally only the super popular kids gave and received the dares. The fact that one of them might have dared me was too crazy to think about. Sure, my sister was a cheerleader when she was in 7th and 8th grade, but that was already three years ago, and everyone had long since learned I was nothing like her.

"Hello? Earth to Bre."

Hearing my name snapped me back to reality. Trent and Penny were both staring at me, waiting for something. Had they asked me a question? Did I accidently speak while I was off in la-la land thinking about the black envelope sitting in my locker?

"What?" I managed, not sure saying anything else was quite safe yet.

"I asked if we're all still going to the dance together." Penny repeated slowly. I had a feeling it wasn't just the second time she was saying these words. "My brother gets the car for the weekend as long as he drives us, so we don't have to walk this time."

"Oh, cool," I said flatly. "I don't know if I want to go, though."

"What do you mean?" Penny exclaimed. "We've been talking about how fun this dance is going to be for months! I mean, it's the last dance before we leave middle school forever. We can't just miss it!"

"Besides," Trent began in a much calmer tone than Penny. "What else are you going to do on a Friday night when both of us are at the dance?"

"Okay, I'll think about it," I said with a sigh.

"Don't think, just say you'll go," Penny demanded. "Please!"

"Fine," was all I managed, my eyes glued to my food. I hoped if I could just focus on the plate in front of me, I could make it through the whole lunch period without incident.

"Bre?"

Looking up I was shocked to see both Trent and Penny were standing up and getting ready to leave the lunch room. Around us, everyone else was also leaving. Somehow I had missed the first bell, and if I didn't hustle, I was going to be late for my next class. Clearly I had focused on my food a little too hard.

"Are you okay?" Trent asked me as we walked to bio a few minutes later. I had thrown away what was left my lunch while Penny gave me an odd look, then decided to skip my locker trip so I didn't have to see the envelope at all. I would deal with the consequences of not having my English book with me later.

"I'm just tired," I lied easily. It was kind of true, though. And even if it wasn't the main reason for my head being in the clouds, it was better than letting Trent know I had a dare in my locker. A massive part of me hoped that when I opened it, the card would be addressed to someone else. Maybe it was just put in the wrong locker. Maybe it was for Frankie who was two lockers down from me. He usually got at least one dare each year. So, maybe I was off the hook.

"Well wake up," Trent smiled. "I can't have my lab partner dozing off today."

With a groan, I marched up the steps to class. How could I have completely forgotten it was dissection day? Before we even entered the classroom, I could smell the chemicals and stench of dead worms. Even without the envelope in my locker factoring in, this was about to be a pretty terrible Tuesday for sure.

Chapter 2

When school was over, I did my best to slip the black envelope into my bag. At that point in the day, I had already done a pretty good job of avoiding both Trent and Penny, so pulling the thin paper out of my locker was rather easy to accomplish. The whole bus ride home, I tried not to make eye contact with anyone, and as soon as the bus stopped at my street, I was sprinting home as fast as I could move.

"Where's the fire?" my sister Caitlyn asked as soon as I slammed through the back door into the kitchen.

"What?" I asked, shocked to see her sitting on the counter waiting for her daily after school pop tart to be ready. "I mean... I'm fine."

"You're so weird," she said with an eye roll and hair flip. She could not be more different than me if she tried.

I raced up to my room then, making sure to not actually run until I was out of eyesight. When I walked into my room I tossed my bag on the floor. It spilled out on my area rug instantly. I watched as the black envelope slid under my desk chair, this time face up. It was the first time I had bothered to look at the front, so seeing it was a whole new shock. Moving closer to stare at it without actually touching it, I saw that my name was written in silver sharpie. I had seen other people's names on envelopes when they had them at school, even my sisters' name on her dares still hanging on her corkboard in her bedroom. But suddenly, actually seeing my name, made me know the envelope had not just been placed in the wrong locker.

Refusing to be in the same room as the dare, I got up and headed to the living room. Knowing there had to be something on TV to help me forget about the dare for a while longer, I snagged some chips on my way, then flopped down on the couch. Unfortunately, just as I was settling into a re-run episode of *Friends*, Caitlyn came into the room chomping loudly on her pop tart.

"Have you seen my new silver flip flops?" she asked between massive bites of her snack. "You used them yesterday, right?"

"No, I had on my grey ones," I corrected her with a sigh. "Last I saw them, yours were in the laundry room."

"I just checked and they're not there," she huffed before turning and storming out of the room.

Trying to get back into the episode, I listened as she stomp-stomped up the steps, clearly not wanting to check in the laundry room as I suggested. Determined to block out the sounds of her feet pounding around while she looked, I turned up the volume on the TV. It was an episode of *Friends* I had seen a few times before but it was still fun to watch and laugh at.

"Look what I found!"

Tearing my eyes off the screen, I was surprised to see Caitlyn standing in the doorway once again. But it was nothing compared to the shock of seeing her holding a familiar black envelope in her hand, instead of her silver flip flops.

"What are you doing?!" I jumped up off of the couch, causing my open bag of chips to spill everywhere. "Why were you in my room?"

"I was looking for my flip flops but found this instead," she said with a massive grin. "Why didn't you open it yet?"

"Give me that!" I grabbed the envelope from her, holding it tight enough to bend it slightly.

"So, open it already!" Caitlyn stepped past me to grab the chips from the floor and take a seat on the couch.

"No," I said with a shake of my head. "I don't want to open it."

"But you have to," she made out between handfuls of food. "If you don't open it then you won't be able to finish the dare."

"I don't want to do this stupid dare anyways," I said with a sigh. "I don't even know how I got nominated in the first place."

"Maybe everyone thinks it's time you start acting like your big sister?" Caitlyn guessed. She had been a cheerleader since she was in 7th grade, and when she got to high school, she went straight to the varsity squad as a freshman. Her boyfriends have always been varsity sports team members, and she is always at the center of every major social event in the school. So, when I chose not to try out for sports in favor of joining the art club and could care less about school functions, everyone was shocked. It was assumed that I would be just like my popular big sister; instead, I was her polar opposite. If it weren't for our matching curly blonde hair and green eyes, everyone would assume I was adopted for sure!

"You know there'll be consequences if you don't finish the dare." Her words brought me out of my head and dropped me back in the present. "When I was in 7th grade, Gary Bronson had to get his head shaved when he didn't kiss Maggie K."

"That's not true," I said, trying to convince myself as well as my sister.

"Sure it is!" Caitlyn insisted. "When I was still in 6th grade, there was a girl that got dared.

After she didn't do her dare, she had to move schools! And when I was in 8th grade, Mr. Mackey failed a kid in gym class for not doing his dare. I mean, who actually fails gym?"

"A teacher can't make someone fail for not kissing someone," I said quickly. "And if someone just says they didn't get their dare then no one can make them pay up for not doing it."

"That's what the dance is for," she said with a smile. "If you don't finish the dare by the start of the dance for whatever reason, whoever dared you is going to make sure everyone knows about it and people won't let you leave until you make good on the dare. And if you don't go to the dance, then they will make you kiss whoever it is during lunch on Monday! Not seeing the dare is not an excuse anyone has ever let slide!"

I didn't want to believe her, but then I remembered how the kiss dare went when I was in 6th grade. Hearing about the dare from my sister, I wasn't too shocked when the black envelopes started showing up around school. Teachers more or less looked the other way since none of the kissing was during class or was too over the top. That was, until Monday. On Monday, a guy actually stood up on a table and had to kiss a girl who joined him there as well. I later found out that she had been sick the week before, so he had to go above and beyond to make up for not completing his dare. Since then, no one stood on tables, but I think that was only since no one actually had the guts to ignore who they were told to kiss.

"You know I'm right," Caitlyn all but laughed. "So just open it and see already! I can give you good ideas on how to surprise him if you want."

"I don't want to open it yet," I finally admitted. "I don't want to get my first kiss this way."

This was an unusual conversation to be having with my sister, but there seemed to be no one else to talk to. If I told Penny, she would make me open the envelope. And if I told Trent he would roll his eyes and send me to talk to Penny. So, I sat down next to my sister, knowing she was no doubt loving the chance to actually have a girl chat with her little sister.

"It's not a big deal Bre," she said, finally setting the chips aside. "The kisses are only five seconds, and as long as one person sees it to verify you actually did it, then you're good. It doesn't have it be in front of everyone if you don't want."

"Five seconds is a long time," I frowned. "And what if I have to kiss someone I don't even know? I mean, I don't hang out with any of the popular kids."

"Which makes it even weirder that you were dared in the first place," Caitlyn pointed out with a confused look. "But don't worry about it. I know girls that had to kiss people they never even talked to. And really, it made it easier. It's hard when it's someone you're in classes with or someone who's dating someone you know."

"Courtney Morris has to kiss an ex-boyfriend," I told her, glad I had the info to add to the conversation.

"Her sister told me at school today." Of course Caitlyn already knew something people at my own school didn't know yet. "Thank goodness you won't have something embarrassing like that for your dare."

"I hope not," I nodded, knowing that without an ex-boyfriend, there was little likelihood of that kind of drama.

"So are you going to open it now?" Caitlyn finally asked, pointing to the envelope I was still clutching in my hands.

"I think I want to wait a little still," I explained. "Maybe the less time I have to worry about it, the less it will stress me out."

"Okay, but don't skip doing it," Caitlyn warned. "It's not worth the consequences for sure. And people will freak if they know my sister refused to do the dare!"

Caitlyn stayed in the living room and joined me watching *Friends*. It was the first time in months that we actually sat in the same room and just hung out. Kind of weird, but also kind of nice. Once the episode that was on ended and a new one began, she headed to her room to call her boyfriend, but not before reminding me one more time that I needed to open the envelope sooner or later.

I chose later, of course. But sadly, not too much later. After talking to Caitlyn, I was having a hard time imagining what I would look like with a shaved head, or how terrible it would be to have to kiss someone on a table in the lunchroom in front of the whole school. I was determined to make it until Thursday before opening the envelope, but instead I finally grabbed it off my nightstand around three in the morning. Sleep was refusing to come until I knew for good.

Tearing open the envelope I pulled out a card that had a familiar rhyme on it. It was the same one they had been using since before Caitlyn was in 7th grade and got her first dare.

"Here is your dare, and here is your mission,
Find your partner, it's time for kissing.
It must be five seconds, and not on the cheek,
But you better hurry, you only have a week.
By the end the of the dance you must finish this dare,
And those who do not... BEWARE!"

I tried not to let the word get to me as I finally opened the card. I was hoping it would tell me to "kiss someone in one of your classes", or "kiss someone that rides on your bus". Even seeing "kiss a football player" or "kiss someone on student council" would have been better that the words I saw before my eyes. I blinked a few times, but the words didn't go away. They just stared at me in bold letters.

"Kiss your best friend."

65446523R00190

Made in the USA
San Bernardino, CA
03 January 2018